Ultimate Game

"He glanced at the rear-view mirror in the car, and saw his face, the heavy, lined face of a sixty–year-old man. Petrified, Charles didn't react when de Marigny handed him the documents, just laid them on his knees without reading them. It wasn't just any face; it was really his own, the face he would have a half-century from now. A face in which he recognized some of his father's and grandfather's features. That sight, more than all the rest, unleashed in him a terrible foreboding, the feeling that something uncanny and terrifying was going on. He knew then, without being able to explain how he was so certain, that he hadn't fallen asleep at the computer, that this was no dream. It was spring, the anguished spring of May 1917, and Charles had crossed to the other side of the screen, into the ultimate experience."

Ultimate Game

a novel by
CHRISTIAN LEHMANN

translated from the French by
WILLIAM RODARMOR

DAVID R. GODINE · Publisher
Boston

First published in 2000 by
DAVID R. GODINE, PUBLISHER, INC.
Post Office Box 450
Jaffrey, New Hampshire 03452
website: www.godine.com

Originally published in French as *No pasarán, le jeu*
by L'Ecole des Loisirs, Paris, in 1996.

Library of Congress Cataloging in Publication Data
Lehmann, Christian.
    [No pasarán, le jeu. English]
    Ultimate game : a novel / by Christian Lehmann ;
    translated from the French by William Rodarmor.
            p.   cm.
    I. Rodarmor, William.   II. Title.
    PQ2672.E4625N613   1999
    843'.914 — dc21   99-23133
                              CIP

ISBN: 1-56792-107-8

First American edition, 2000

Printed on acid-free paper
in the United States of America

Ultimate Game

It was a miracle they found the store at all. Charles had made the mistake of scribbling the address on the back of his Underground ticket, not realizing that here in London he'd have to give the ticket to the collector at the exit gate. At the top of the escalator, the three French boys found themselves caught in the crowd surging toward the gate.

"You have to hand in your ticket!" yelled Andreas. "I *told* you to write it down somewhere else! You're such a moron!"

Meanwhile, Eric tried to memorize the address: "Games Frenzy! 125 Upper Tollington Court Road."

The boys had noticed the phrase earlier in the day. "GAMES FRENZY!" screamed a crudely printed flyer stuck over a poster for Bruce Willis's latest action film. Eric had been the first to spot it: "Hey, guys, get a load of this."

Andreas and Charles, who were a few steps ahead of him on the platform, turned around and stopped amid the stream of passengers. Eric glanced at his friends to make sure they'd heard him, then stood against the wall to let the crowd by. Charles stepped aside for a lady carrying a child, but Andreas marched straight back, jostling two or three people without apologizing. At seventeen, he was a colossus, standing a good shaved head taller than most of the other passengers. One of them, a man of about forty, turned around to complain, but changed his mind when his eyes met Andreas's.

"What have you found, geek?" said Andreas, standing in front of Eric.

"An advertisement! An ad for a games store that looks totally awesome."

"Oh, yeah?"

Andreas peered at the flyer with interest, trying to understand it. Andreas was terrible at English — as at most other subjects, for that matter — and to avoid rubbing it in, Eric gave a rough translation into their native French:

"'*Frénésie du Jeu*' — that's the name of the store — 'A few minutes from the Underground in the heart of London, the shop you've always dreamed of! All the games, for all platforms, at the best prices! Game Boy, PlayStation, CD-ROM. Everything in stock! Bargain-basement prices! Bonus for all purchases of twenty pounds or more: an original CD-ROM with all the best levels of *Doom*.'"

"*Doooooommmm*," murmured Andreas, rolling his eyes.

"Don't expect me to go there with you," Charles

piped up. "From the looks of that flyer, I'll bet it's a pretty cheesy operation. They probably sell nothing but pirated stuff, and you can get five years in jail for that."

"*Doooooommmm*," Andreas repeated on a lower note, advancing on Charles's throat with claw-like hands.

"Stop acting like an idiot! Someone'll see us."

After walking around London all day, Eric was tired. He was tired of Andreas's jokes and tired of Charles's constant complaints. For a moment, he thought about Elena, and wondered where she was now. It was their second and next-to-last day in London before going home to Paris. Yesterday they had visited Tower Bridge, the Tower of London, and Madame Tussaud's Wax Museum. Andreas had especially enjoyed the Chamber of Horrors, and even Eric admitted to a certain fascination as they wandered through a reconstruction of the alleyways once haunted by Jack the Ripper. But today's program was something else again. Taking advantage of the class being split into two groups, Andreas and Eric had figured out how to escape their teachers' vigilance and avoid having to tour Westminster Abbey and the Houses of Parliament.

Then, just as their classmates were boarding the two buses chartered by the school, Andreas had grabbed Charles and dragged him into the dormitory bathroom while Eric stood watch.

"You're coming with us! We're going to spend the day walking around London, nice and easy, without any teachers."

"You're crazy! Someone will notice. And I want to see the... *oww!*"

Andreas raked his knuckles fast across the top of Charles's skull, right where it would hurt the most, then stroked the younger boy's forehead consolingly.

"You should be grateful to us, dude. Thanks to us, you're about to spend the best day of your miserable little life."

"But I promised my mom I'd bring her some postcards of Westminster Abbey. And besides..."

"Hey, come off it! You aren't going to start *bawling* now, are you?" Looking disgusted, Andreas released him. "Your two best friends are trying to cut you in on the best scheme in school history, and you're gonna let them down? Too bad for you, dude. Can't say we didn't try."

Charles looked pleadingly at Eric, trying to convince his schoolmate that the plan was crazy, but Eric, hidden behind the partly open bathroom door, looked away. At that moment, he caught a glimpse of Elena at the end of the hall, silhouetted in a ray of sunshine. Something exploded in his chest, and

6

he suddenly went weak in the knees. She disappeared outside. Eric turned, dimly aware of Charles pulling at his sleeve.

"Tell him this is a stupid idea!" Charles urged. "If a teacher sees we're missing..."

"Andreas crossed our names off both lists last night," Eric explained calmly. "Each teacher will assume we're in the other's group."

"But what about this *evening*?" asked Charles, jerkily resetting his glasses. "Have you thought about this evening? If the teachers get to talking..."

"Oh, I don't believe this," grumbled Andreas. "Go stick your head in the toilet and flush it. You're such a drag."

Eric stepped aside and opened the door to let his friend by. Charles's confusion was comical.

"Don't misunderstand me, guys. It's not that I don't appreciate the thought. But if anyone notices and squeals on us..."

Andreas snorted, his mouth twisted into a sardonic grin. "Squeal on *me*? You know many kids in the class who want to die young?"

Outside, the bus engine roared to life, and they heard the front door creak shut.

Charles took a few steps, then turned back to them, as if to make one last excuse. His lips were trembling.

Eric took pity on him, and was about to say it was no big deal and no hard feelings, when Charles suddenly ripped off his cap and scarf, threw them down, and yelled, "All right! All right! I'm coming with you! To hell with postcards of Westminster Abbey."

Andreas patted him affectionately on the shoulder. "See, sweetie pie? Where there's a will, there's a way."

2

As the crowd swept them toward the Underground exit, Eric feverishly tried to memorize the address: "125 Upper Tollington Court Road." The idea of coming all this way only to fail so close to their goal was driving him crazy.

The ticket collector took their stubs without so much as a nod, and Eric felt the familiar feeling of rage and impotence that the adult world often provoked in him. They climbed an endless stairway — Eric thought the London Underground was probably deep enough in places to reach the outskirts of Hell — and finally came out into the open air under a darkened sky. In the space of the half-hour it had taken to travel to Sainsbury Park in north London, the afternoon had turned gloomily overcast.

"Oh, man!" groaned Charles. "We'll never make it back in time."

Andreas grabbed him by the collar and propelled him gently forward, Charles's feet barely touching the ground.

"We're almost there. It'd be dumb to turn around now."

"He's right," said Eric. "It's just a few minutes from the Tube."

Catching his friends' eyes, Eric saw that they, too, even Charles, shared the same eagerness. A new store, with unsuspected treasures! Deep down, he tried to steel himself against disappointment. In spite of the promises in the flyer, the store would probably only have a few last copies of some out-dated games. But for the moment, anything was possible, everything belonged to the world of magic. Though they were teenagers, all three boys felt themselves carried back in time to those feverish Christmas mornings when they had tried hard not to start shouting for joy. As the years passed, those little epiphanies became less frequent, and — observing his brother Gilles and his mother — Eric sensed bitterly that things would only get worse. With age, those moments of pure happiness became rarer, to one day disappear. "Then I'll really be an adult," he said to himself when he was feeling down. The thought made him sick.

They walked quickly through the neighborhood around the Underground station, climbed a steep hill, glanced into alleyways. The few shops they saw sharpened their determination: exotic-looking stores touting miracle hair-growing lotions, electronics shops with carcasses of hi-fi systems stacked on the sidewalk under misspelled signs, tiny post offices with grimy windows. The boys had spent twenty minutes crisscrossing the area and were drenched in sweat. But they were determined not to ask help from a passerby, partly out of stubbornness, partly because none of them felt able to pronounce the complicated address in English. If only the shop were on Dog Street or Milk Lane, instead of...

"Lower Tollington Court Road!" Charles shouted, pointing toward a small, ivy-covered sign.

"So what?" grumbled Andreas. "That's not the one we're looking for."

"No, but listen: if it's Lower Tollington, then Upper Tollington can't be far away. We must be very close."

"We may be close, but it's a quarter to six. I bet we'll find the place shut."

With the energy of despair, they started running up the middle of Lower Tollington Court Road, stopping at each intersection, only to go on again, disappointed. They had covered nearly a mile in a long curve, when, walking aimlessly, Eric stepped on a handbill that stuck to his shoe. He almost slipped on the wet asphalt, and bent down to pull off the paper. For a moment, as if in a cartoon, his eyes widened as he read the few letters visible beneath the smear from his muddy shoe: "Games Fr..." with a sketch of the neighborhood.

"I've got it! I've got it!" he shouted, but the wind carried the handbill away, and Andreas had to catch him before he stumbled and fell.

"The paper!" screamed an agitated Eric, as his companions stared at him in bewilderment.

A gust caught the dirty sheet of paper and carried it aloft. Watching it, Eric stepped onto the street. A passing car grazed him, splashing his shoes with freezing water, but he took no notice, just crossed the street like a zombie, followed by his two comrades. The handbill caught on the branches of a tree, then slipped to the ground, only to zip between two parked cars and blow down an alley. The three boys turned the street corner, muttering incoherent curses.

The store was flanked by two abandoned warehouses. The handbill blew against the glass door for a moment, then went on its way in the darkness. Dumb with amazement, Eric, Andreas, and Charles advanced like automatons toward the illuminated store window, their eyes drawn by brightly colored game boxes and dazzling posters. Here, under the *Mechwarrior 2* logo, a killer robot ten stories tall emerged from a sea of flames and explosions. There, a chaos warrior in a loincloth swung a two-handed sword, splitting the skulls of a half-dozen slavering orcs. Here again, two green-haired creatures on an invisible spring climbed up and down the plate-glass window while holding a multi-colored umbrella.

"This is seriously weird," breathed Andreas. "This is usually the point where I wake up."

But it was no dream. The doorknob was solid enough, and the door even stuck for a moment. Eric shoved with all his might, and it opened. He recognized the smell of the shop. It was the smell of Christmas mornings, of shiny cellophane under torn gift wrap, boxes full of things that were clean, new, and unknown. For a moment, the three stood together on the threshold as if reluctant to break the magic spell of the place, then slowly and hesitantly, they split up.

Charles slowly took off his cap and scarf. Eric watched him out of the corner of his eye, thinking it was probably because of the heat in the shop, but it was like watching a believer enter a church. Eric stared at the display in front of him, slowly reaching for a game even as he delayed the moment of contact. This is stupid, he briefly thought. These are computer games, not the Holy Grail. But the thought only grazed his mind, and he picked up the box cautiously, almost with reverence. Inside the shop, time stood still.

"Take a look at this," whispered Charles.

Pulled from his daydream, Eric turned to his classmate. The three of them were the only customers in the store.

"'*Fall of Stalingrad:* A revolutionary strategy game, based on the 1942 German siege of the Russian city. Featuring hyper-real simulation of weather conditions, encyclopedic listings of all armaments available to each side, and a hyper-real index of despair and famine among the besieged.' I didn't even know this was out. What have you found?"

"It's the sequel to *Flashback*. You know, the adventures of Conrad Hart. At the end of the last episode he's captured by the Morphs of Evil, but is freed by the chief of the Resistance of Good's daughter…"

Under his breath, Eric was translating at fever pitch.

"It's called *Fade to Black* and it has loads of new technical features. 'The previous game platform has been replaced by an incredible adventure with fourteen levels of play, in three dimensions, with changing points of view during encounters with the space warriors.'"

"This looks so cool," commented Charles.

But Eric grimaced.

"What's the matter?"

"Have you seen the prices?"

Charles turned the box over and inspected its sides, in vain.

"There *aren't* any prices."

"That's right," said Eric. "Which means only one thing. Everything here is brand-new. There's no swap counter, nothing on sale, just the latest stuff. Some of it isn't even supposed to be available in Europe yet. Look," he said, pointing to the boxes of *Ultima XII* and *Quake III*. "They must be imported directly from the States. I've looked through every French and English magazine I could find, and I still didn't know some of those games existed, or that they were being developed. Believe me, we must be in a super-specialized store, and if the prices aren't marked on the boxes, it's because..." Eric mimed hitting himself over the head with a hammer.

"Listen," Charles broke in. "All we have to do is ask."

"I only have twenty pounds," Eric finally admitted.

He was about to put the box back onto the display case, but Charles grabbed it.

"Check on the price first, and if you're a bit short..."

He turned around to the counter, cutting off Eric's half-spoken thanks.

*   *   *

Andreas, squatting in front of a display case, seemed to have forgotten the other two. Unable to read the English text, he stared at the cover artwork and turned the boxes over to examine the little screen shots, trying to imagine what the scenes of carnage he enjoyed so much would look like on his big seventeen-inch monitor. Since 1994, a new regulation in the United States had required that each game be rated according to its violence level. But this had quickly been subverted by the designers of the most brutal games, who were only too happy to promote a range of storylines, each more vicious than the next. Advertisements in the game magazines twisted the rule further, lauding each new level of gore as a blow for freedom of speech. While pretending to obey the law, some game publishers now included settings that let you choose your preferred level of butchery.

Andreas loved to push things to the limit immediately, calling his two less bloodthirsty friends cowards. He boasted to anyone who would listen that he'd finished *the* ultimate game, *Doom*, at maximum violence level, without using any cheat codes, invulnerability, or extra weapons or ammunition. Eric wondered if that were possible. It wasn't very comforting to picture Andreas at night, alone in front of his screen, headphones on, roaming the endless levels of *Doom* with a rocket launcher in his hand, striding through the splattered brains of his enemies, with that strange glitter in his eye Eric had sometimes seen.

The man behind the counter didn't look at all the way Eric would have imagined. Most computer-game store owners were players themselves, or ex-players, plugged into the world of games since childhood. Few were past their forties. Eric knew a couple of players and store owners who were older, of course. Some were even close to sixty, a fact that Eric, who couldn't imagine ever stopping playing, found unconsciously reassuring for his future. With age, however, these few venerable ancients usually turned to pure strategy games of the kind that Charles liked, or role-playing or adventure games, full of the hobbits and elfin creatures that would make Andreas want to vomit.

The man at the counter must have been almost eighty. Wearing a raspberry-colored sweater that did-n't quite hide his frayed shirt, he seemed to be doz-ing behind the cash register. A large newspaper was open on his knees. Over the years, steaming mugs of tea had left a series of dark circles on the wooden counter. Eric thought briefly of Sleeping Beauty.

"Pardon me, sir," Charles began in a shy voice, speaking nearly perfect English.

The man raised his eyes, but his glasses and bushy eyebrows hid his gaze.

"Can you tell me how much these articles cost?"

Eric stifled a laugh. Charles had memorized the taped English lessons that Mrs. Levine had inflicted on them for the last three years, and he could perfectly mimic the tone of the recording, provided he didn't have to make any real effort of syntax or imagination.

"Certainly," said the old man. "Isn't the price marked on them?"

Eric's cheeks reddened and his heart started to pound. He obviously doesn't know a damned thing, he thought. The old guy is clueless. He's probably just here to mind the store until closing time.

The same thought must have occurred to Charles, who shot him a covert glance.

The old man reached his hand over the counter and Charles surrendered the game boxes to him. The man coughed, adjusted his glasses, and very slowly turned the boxes over.

"Quite so, the prices aren't marked..."

Still very slowly, the old man drew a cloth-covered order book from the cash register and consulted a list of titles. Eric thought that using such an old-fashioned, inefficient system in a computer store was really too much. He suddenly realized that there wasn't a single computer in the entire store. Not on the counter, to log in orders and purchases, not in the window, not even for demos.

"I don't see them on my stock list," said the old man with a look of annoyance.

The two boys remained silent.

"If you come back tomorrow, I might…"

"We're French," said Charles. "We're going home tomorrow with our school."

"French?" asked the old man.

Something glinted in his eyes.

"Well look, because this is a somewhat unusual situation, I'll let you have them at the sale price, five pounds ninety-nine each."

At that price, these games cost less than old copies of unplayable games from the eighties. Either the old man was *really* clueless, or this store was the most amazing place on the planet.

"Thank you very much," said Eric and Charles in unison. Their voices quavered slightly. They felt really grateful to the old man, but it was mixed with the unpleasant feeling that they were taking advantage of him.

The two games vanished into a paper bag. Eric realized that at those prices he could clean out the shop, but he didn't dare add anything more. He was handing a bank note to the old man when Andreas reappeared.

"Shit, this is too good to be true! Look what I found: *Mortal Kombat 5!* Check out the screens."

He pushed the black box with its reddish streaks at Eric, who glimpsed a few bloody scenes that were at once implausible and thoroughly revolting.

"Ask him what the price is," Andreas commanded.

Charles did; the old man reached his hand out for the box and inspected it.

"It's thirty-nine pounds and ninety-nine pence."

"Damn, that's pretty steep… Can you lend me ten pounds?"

Charles hesitated.

"Come on, don't be a jerk. You don't come across a deal like this every day."

Charles drew ten pounds from his pocket and added them to Andreas's thirty. But just when the transaction was almost complete, the old man suddenly stiffened. Eric thought he was having an attack and got ready to help, but the man looked Andreas right in the eye and asked in a loud voice, "What is *that?*"

Baffled, the three schoolmates fell silent.

"I beg your pardon?" asked Charles timidly.

The man reached over the counter, grabbed Andreas's leather bomber jacket, and repeated his question. He was jabbing his index finger at one of the metal insignias Andreas wore as a decoration.

Stunned, Eric watched the scene. The old man was radiating energy and anger that belied his age. Eric noticed a tattoo on the man's forearm that the shirt sleeve didn't quite hide, a few black numbers lost in a forest of age-whitened hairs.

"The old fart's out of his mind," Andreas protested as he struggled to get free.

He jerked sharply backward, not daring to grab the old man's arm. The leather of his jacket tore with a ripping sound and the metal insignia fell to the floor.

"What a dick!" Andreas raged between clenched teeth.

He stooped, picked up the raptor-headed insignia, and clutched it in his hand.

"Do you know what that insignia stands for?" asked the old man, livid.

Charles translated, awkwardly, for Andreas's benefit. To his two friends' great surprise, Andreas hesitated and blushed, then silently shrugged his shoulders.

Before any of them could react, he spun on his heel, shoved the glass door open, and stormed out of the shop, holding the game to his chest. Charles and Eric hesitated, then turned to look at the shop-keeper with curiosity.

The man was leaning against a wall, shakily rubbing his forehead.

"It will never end," he murmured.

Charles took a step backward, silently tugging on Eric's sleeve to get him to leave the store, but Eric gestured for him to wait.

"Are you all right, sir?" asked Eric.

As if suddenly aware that they were still there, the old man raised his eyes to the two boys.

"Do you know what that was?"

They didn't answer.

"That symbol, do you know what it stands for? Does your friend know?"

Eric shrugged his shoulders, to convey his ignorance.

The old man shook his head. He seemed exhausted, defeated.

"How old are you?" he asked.

"Fifteen," answered Charles. "Well, that is, we are. Our friend is seventeen."

"Fifteen years old..." repeated the old man.

He leaned against the counter, opened a cabinet, and bent down to retrieve a dusty game box.

"Here," he said, putting it into Eric's hands.

"What is it?"

"It's a game, young man. A game you have never played before."

Eric and Charles discreetly looked the box over. It was black, a bit smaller than usual, and had no label. Shaking it slightly, Eric could feel its contents shift. The box was very light; it couldn't contain more than a diskette or two, maybe not even an instruction manual.

"What's it called?" asked Charles.

"On your way, now. I have to close up." With a weary gesture, the old man pointed them toward the door. "Play it with your friend. Especially with him. If it isn't too late."

"He's lost it," mumbled Charles as they went out the door.

Eric paid no attention. He was backing away, his eyes fixed on the old man lost in the depths of the store. Eric heard him murmur one more time, as if to himself, "It will never end."

They found Andreas on the Underground platform.

"What a psycho that old guy was," he spat as they approached.

"So what *is* that thing, that insignia?" asked Eric.

"What do you care?"

23

"Don't be that way. Why don't you at least show it to us?"

"Do I quiz you about the stuff *you* wear? Do I ask if you're still wearing Bart Simpson underpants?"

"Hey, come on, stop it, both of you," Charles said. "Let's not fight over such a little thing. The old man just lost it, that's all."

Andreas promptly enlisted him. "See what I mean? Truth from the mouths of dwarves."

The train approached with a characteristic screech. They stepped aboard, along with a pigeon that was hopping along the platform and seemed to have decided to change stations. As soon as Andreas was seated, he pulled the *Mortal Kombat* 5 box from his bag and stroked the cellophane shrink-wrap.

"This is so totally cool," he said, before pulling out a pocket knife and slitting the wrapping.

He opened the box. The CD-ROM appeared, a shiny metallic disc displaying a dragon's head floating on a pool of scarlet blood.

"Holy shit…" muttered Andreas before starting to leaf through the thick instruction manual.

For his part, Eric had taken out the black cardboard box the old man had given him and lifted the lid. He wasn't sure exactly what he expected, since he had deliberately refused to imagine what kind of game the box might contain. But he couldn't help feeling a sharp pang of disappointment when he saw the brief instruction sheet and a single 3.5-inch diskette.

3

"YOU'RE REALLY in hot water, guys. Old lady Levine suspects something's up."

Alexander, who had come out to warn them, had been waiting in the priory garden for an hour.

"How long have you been back?"

"At least two hours. The teachers had time to compare their lists and saw that three kids were missing from the Westminster Abbey group. But you lucked out: Mrs. Machez forgot to call roll, so they don't know exactly who played hookey."

"So there's no problem, then," said Andreas.

"Wait a minute," said Eric. "Not so fast. Give me a minute to think." To Alexander, he said, "Tell us what you did today, where you had lunch, the whole deal."

Alexander was only too happy to help them out. Among their schoolmates, Eric, Charles, and Andreas were known as the Joystick Aces, because they were the only ones with powerful, cutting-edge computers. The three friends wore their technical edge like a halo. They were the first to try out the latest games, and the first to discover their subtleties, flaws, and shortcuts.

When Alexander finished describing his day,

they gave him the game boxes to smuggle into the dormitory once the coast was clear. Andreas decided to spend a few more minutes outside, but Eric and Charles went on ahead. They had just reached the dormitory door when Mrs. Levine's voice rang out.

"Boisdeffre, Martineau! Come here a minute."

They froze, then slowly turned. Charles had gone pale.

"Yes, ma'am," said Eric, taking the lead.

The English teacher was standing in the doorway to her room at the end of the hallway.

Struggling to master his rising panic, Eric slowly walked toward her. Charles followed, dragging his feet. Even at this snail's pace, Eric thought to himself, we'll soon be face-to-face with her. He desperately tried to think of a way to avoid the encounter, but couldn't come up with anything that might work.

He was less than ten yards from Mrs. Levine when the door to the girls' dormitory suddenly swung open, caught Eric full tilt, and slammed him against the wall. He collapsed under the impact and stars danced before his eyes. He could hear his teacher shouting, a cry that seemed to come from very far away. When he opened his eyes, Elena was leaning over him.

"I'm so sorry," she said in the strange accent that had haunted Eric's nights since he'd first heard it. "I'm so terribly sorry."

"You must be out of your mind, running into the hallway like that," fumed Mrs. Levine.

Eric tried to smile, to show that it was no big deal, but he could only stare at her, and then was baffled to feel Elena's hand in his jacket pocket.

She stood up and faced Mrs. Levine, who pushed her aside to examine Eric. Reassured to see that he bore no signs of injury, she helped him to his feet. He was so astonished at Elena's gesture that he didn't even think to pretend to be hurt. The door's rubber sheathing had absorbed the shock, and he felt only a vague soreness in his left arm.

"You seem to be all right," said Mrs. Levine, more as an order than a statement. "Come with me into the office."

They obeyed, and found themselves in the small room where she had set up her bedroom for the three days of the trip. Eric glimpsed a lacy night-gown under the pillow and a crossword-puzzle magazine sticking out of a wicker basket, and was intrigued by these clues to his teacher's life.

"Did you spend a pleasant afternoon?" asked Mrs. Levine, leaning against a chest of drawers.

Charles tried to answer too quickly, and got choked up.

"It was very nice, ma'am," said Eric. "Really great."

"Was there something you especially liked during your visit? Something that you'll keep as a treasured memory?"

"The Abbey museum, ma'am. I really enjoyed the pictures of medieval life. The toy soldiers and all."

"Is that so? What about you, Boisdeffre?"

"The cider ice cream that the Italian ice-cream man sold outside the Abbey… I mean, the library…"

Mrs. Levine was looking them over. Eric felt she was about to pounce, that the slightest slip on their part would send them careening into the abyss of detention or expulsion. Trying to act casual, Eric stuck his hand in his pocket, where it met a stiff cardboard rectangle.

"Was Westminster Abbey the way you imagined it?" asked Mrs. Levine.

Charles hesitated, screwing up his face as if the complexity of the question demanded careful thought. In a flash of insight, Eric drew his hand from his pocket, and pointed blindly at the postcard it now held.

"This is what I found especially strange," he said.

Mrs. Levine leaned over to see. Eric's finger had landed on the lawn in front of the building.

"The grass? You found the grass strange?"

Eric lifted his finger, revealing the remains of a cross stuck in the ground.

"No, no, not the grass. The old tombs, the…"

"The Celtic crosses," Charles prompted.

At a loss, Mrs. Levine looked at them for a moment, then sighed.

The trip back to Paris unfolded without major incident. Eric spent the two-hour ferry passage from Dover to Calais stuck to an uncomfortable leather chair in the video room, watching an endless loop of Walt Disney cartoons. But Donald and Goofy's antics rarely held his attention. He only had eyes for Elena, who was sitting a few rows away with a half-dozen girlfriends. He watched her profile turned toward the television and the bright sparkle of her teeth when she laughed, which was often. Once in a while, she brushed her hair away from her forehead, revealing her face, and Eric felt an intense desire to do something, anything, without quite knowing what that was. He had the vague, impossible notion that she knew he was spying on her, and that she was doing that business with her hair with him personally in mind. The very next moment, he was struck by the complete stupidity of the thought. So he sat there, nailed to the spot, trying to keep his knees from shaking.

Charles had allowed Andreas to drag him into the saloon bar. Using his friend's last pound notes, Andreas had no difficulty ordering two pints of beer, which they drank slowly on the windswept aft deck, far from prying eyes. Charles didn't finish his glass, however. Shortly before their arrival at Calais, he abruptly stood up, rushed to the railing, and generously drenched the side of the ferry with half-digested beer. Greenish and nauseated, he watched as the sea gulls dove toward the sea below, only to wing away swiftly, screeching in disappointment.

Despite a stream of jibes and dirty jokes from Andreas, Charles and Eric remained silent all the way to Paris. When they parted in front of their school four hours later, he treated each of them to a stinging punch on the arm.

"So long, losers! With one of you puking and the other in love, I can't say this has been one of the all-time great trips."

They separated, thinking about the next day, their upcoming classes, and especially the math test that had loomed over them for the past week. They'd managed to forget all about it during the whole trip, but now it weighed heavily on their minds. None of them gave the games store another thought.

4

THE APARTMENT LAY in darkness. Eric put his suitcase down and walked to his mother's room, guided by the sound of canned laughter. The television sat on a chest of drawers at the foot of the bed, surrounded by a heap of carefully labeled video cassettes and filling the room with bluish light. Eric leaned over and smiled at his mother. She gave him a kiss and stroked his cheek.

"Did you have a nice trip?"

"Yeah, it was great."

"Your brother made something to eat. I think there's still some chicken in the refrigerator."

"Gilles is home?"

"He's on leave until next Friday."

"Is this the famous leave he was supposed to have last summer?"

"That's what he said. He put his things in your room."

Eric turned and was about to leave.

"Stay a little longer. Gilles went out with some friends. He'll be back late."

Eric sat down at the foot of the bed. "England was really great…"

His mother gave a little smile and cut him off.

"Not now, darling. The show's almost over."

Eric nodded, letting his gaze roam around the room. Old *TV Guides* were piled on the floor between the bed and the window. Eric leaned over to pick up one of the magazines, taking care not to disturb the dozens of tiny vials of homeopathic remedies that his mother had strewn on the night table. He settled at the foot of the bed and began paging through it, his mind elsewhere.

5

THE SHOTGUN WAS out of ammunition. Andreas hit the 5 key, got the rocket launcher, and ran across the street. A fireball drifted his way from the top of a building, but he paid no attention. As long as he kept moving, the demons had no chance of hitting him at that distance. He spun around to make sure no monsters were sneaking up behind him, then continued running toward the central building. Once inside, he hit 4, temporarily swapping his rocket launcher for the shotgun. Rockets were much too dangerous in close combat. If one exploded nearby, or if he fired too close to a wall, he would be burned to a crisp. And he was so near his goal…

Andreas had been playing *Doom* for the last three hours. Fatigue was gaining on him in spite of the excitement, but he had set himself the goal of reaching the end of this level in one session, without saving the game or using any cheat codes. His health was at 67 percent and his armor at 88 percent, and he'd been able to pick up a blue key without too much trouble. His ammunition was okay, except for bullets, so his first goal was to find a case of them as soon as possible. When he was inside a darkened building like this one, the double-barreled shotgun was his favorite weapon. True, it took a little longer to reload than the single-barreled one, but its firepower was more deadly, especially at point-blank range.

He settled into a corner of the building near a gigantic staircase, waited a few seconds to make sure no monster had detected his movements, then released the mouse just long enough to grab his can and swallow the last of his beer. He was still thirsty, but he didn't want to leave the screen to go to the kitchen. In that situation, any other player would have hit the <Escape> key to pause the game, but that was one of the crutches that real Fragmeisters disdained. Andreas glanced at his alarm clock. One o'clock in the morning... It was time to wrap things up. He toyed with the handle of his hunting knife, lightly rubbing the blade across his bare thigh.

An inhuman roaring rose from the building's depths. Andreas put the knife down and confidently grabbed the mouse. With his left hand, he pounded the direction arrows on the keyboard, moving him forward. He turned, and his field of vision revealed the huge stairway, with a horde of imps crowding the top and a dozen lost souls floating over them. When the mob caught sight of him, it roared and started tumbling down the stairs. Andreas hesitated a fraction of a second. His left ring finger hit the 6 key, the plasma gun appeared in his hands, and he rushed forward to meet the horde. He pressed the left mouse button, and bursts of pure energy shot out in front of him, opening a path with a shower of emerald-green sparks. Pulverized at point-blank range, the imps exploded with screams of rage. But their number slowed Andreas down, allowing the more cunning ones to attack him from behind. One of them managed to slash him with a horn, and for a moment the screen turned blood-red, as his face at the bottom of the screen grimaced in pain. He spun round, blasted the area around him clear, then continued climbing. He had almost reached the top of the stairs when one of the lost souls rushed at him with a sinister screech. Avoiding the fiery maw at the last second, he reached the landing at the top of the stairs. Caught in the crossfire behind him, the imps and the lost souls were tearing each other apart. On his left, Andreas spotted a narrow corridor. As he ran toward it, he glimpsed a box of bullets out of the corner of his eye. He angled to the right and picked it up. The Gatling gun appeared in his hands with a sharp click that made Andreas smile in the darkness.

He continued left toward the corridor, firing two bursts in the general direction of the stairs. An imp was blasted into the air and fell out of sight. Andreas had almost reached the mouth of the corridor when he heard an awesome trumpeting on his right. A huge panel opened in the wall, revealing a hell knight in all his maleficent splendor. Andreas was so startled, he knocked his empty beer can to the floor. His left hand skidded across the keyboard, hitting the 6 key while he pressed the left mouse button. The Gatling gun barked, sending a cloud of lead into the monster's monumental legs from close range. Then the plasma gun appeared almost instantly, and Andreas, his finger still curled on the mouse, engulfed the hell knight in a torrent of pure energy.

Alarmed at how close the monster was, he glanced at the bottom of the screen and was horrified to see that all his stats were dropping. His weapon's ammo supply was plummeting, but that was normal. What stunned him was to see that his health and armor points were disappearing as well. Something was attacking him! Something was slashing at him from behind! He gritted his teeth, choking back a cry of rage and disappointment. The hell knight finally collapsed, and Andreas began to turn around. But before he could make it, his health fell to zero percent and he slumped to the ground in a pool of blood.

In the instant before passing out, he glimpsed

the hind legs of the imp that had just killed him. Andreas felt a burst of rage. To have faced a hell knight and a horde of demons only to fall into the claws of a mere imp whom he could normally kill with his bare hands in an open field...! The words "Game Over" appeared on the screen in red letters. Andreas grabbed the knife and jabbed it into the wood of his computer table. He closed his eyes and heaved a deep sigh. "Take it easy," he told himself. "A real Fragmeister doesn't get discouraged. Death in combat is the most beautiful death..."

Andreas couldn't remember where he had read that, and he wasn't even sure what "Fragmeister" meant. Charles claimed it was just a German-sounding title that some British *Doom* champion had given himself after beating hundreds of competitors in networked tournaments. But Andreas was sure it meant something else, some message only he could decipher. He opened his eyes again. His gaze ran over the posters on the wall and the big red silk sheet on which he'd pinned most of his collection of medals and military insignia. From the bureau, he picked up the death's-head insignia, stroked the pin that the crazy old man had bent...

A twisted grin creased Andreas's face. Ignoring the alarm clock, which now read 1:30 A.M., he turned back to the screen and keyed in "New

Game." He found himself at the start of a level in the corner of a room full of devils and zombie-commandoes. On the keyboard, his fingers tapped out a first code, IDKFA. His ammunition and armor levels rose to maximum. Then he typed in IDDAD, a code he used very rarely. His face at the bottom of the screen underwent a dramatic change, with rays of green energy now shining from his eyes. His mouth dry, Andreas pressed the 1 key and the chain saw appeared in his hands. For a few moments, he savored the familiar rumble of its well-oiled motor, then closed his eyes and rushed to the center of the crowded room. The chain saw's roar rose in pitch as it cut into his enemies' flesh. Deliberately keeping his eyes closed, Andreas turned in a circle, ripping the waves of attackers, who fell at his feet amid fountains of scarlet blood. When the last roars of pain fell silent, Andreas opened his eyes and surveyed the carnage. His health and armor were still at maximum. He lowered the saw and heaved a sigh of immense satisfaction… It wasn't something to do too often, of course, but Andreas really, really loved relaxing in "God" mode.

6

THE ALARM WOKE Eric at seven. Gilles hadn't come in last night. Eric stepped across his brother's empty folding cot and got dressed, his mind still in a fog. He had dreamed about Elena that night, but the memory was fading. Eric quickly glanced at his brother's things, looking in vain for a men's magazine. A book lay on the night table next to an overflowing ashtray. He picked it up, read the title: *Man's Hope* by André Malraux. On the cover, smiling soldiers leaned from the windows of a departing train and punched their fists in the air. Eric glanced at the back-cover blurb: it was about an attack against a rebel-held fort somewhere in Spain. A war story, obviously, though in his letters Gilles had sounded sick and tired of war. He had volunteered to serve in Bosnia but seemed to have lost his illusions as the months went by.

As Eric put the book down, a photo fell out from between its pages. It was a Polaroid snapshot showing an armored truck and a pile of sandbags in the background. In the foreground stood two blond children, a boy and a girl of about ten, dressed in brightly colored sweaters, coarse canvas pants, and red rubber boots. They were eating candy and grinning happily. The girl was laughing and holding her doll out to the camera; it was a Barbie doll, its top held together by a generous amount of adhesive tape. Eric slipped the photograph back into the book and went to brush his teeth. He had spent the previous evening desperately going over his last math assignments, and his head was still crammed with half-understood formulas. But he was struck by the sudden thought that he needed to find out more about his brother, and what he had seen over there.

Eric finished his coffee and looked at his watch. He still had a quarter of an hour before the next bus to school. He hesitated, listening carefully. His mother was still asleep; he could hear her regular breathing. When he was younger, after his father had left them and nightmares drove him from his bed, he would often spend the rest of the night with her. In those days, his mother's warm breath and the mist of medications and vaporizers would comfort him and help him fall asleep. Nowadays, things were different. Mother hadn't left the apartment for the last four months, despite Dr. Munier's urging. Eric had started avoiding him. He would lie low when the doctor was called to the house, afraid of having to meet his concerned look and probing questions. He dreaded hearing the doctor say that

Mother was seriously ill, or, perhaps even worse, that there was nothing wrong with her.

He checked to be sure his school bag was ready, sat down at the computer, and put the alarm clock where he could see it. A quarter of an hour... He probably didn't have time to install the *Fade to Black* CD-ROM and set the sound and visual parameters. Besides, he wanted to take his time and enjoy learning his new game bit by bit. But there was no reason why he shouldn't check out the program the old English shopkeeper had slipped him. A game that could fit on a single diskette was probably older and pretty primitive. It would take no more time to install than it would to erase from his hard disk if it didn't turn out to be worthwhile. Eric switched his brother's computer on, waited while the machine booted up, and watched as the lines of its internal program scrolled by until the ready "C:\" prompt appeared. Eric pushed the single diskette into the drive and typed "A:\".

The instruction sheet bore only the usual warnings about epilepsy, which he didn't bother reading. He typed "install," then hit <Enter>, without result. He tried "play" followed by <Enter>. Nothing happened. He was about to check the diskette's file directory by typing "dir" when the computer gave an outraged whine and crashed.

That sort of thing had happened before, and Eric was pretty sure he knew what to do: press the reset button to avoid damaging the computer's fragile electronic components, and erase the offending program or programs. But he hesitated for a moment, mesmerized by a succession of incomprehensible lines of code that were sweeping across the screen. Then he grew alarmed. A virus! The diskette was infected, and he had just introduced a virus into his brother's computer! In a panic, he punched the power switch, shutting off the computer's central processing unit, screen, and speakers with an ugly electronic crunch. He then forced himself to wait for thirty seconds, as all the computer manuals recommended. Eric could imagine the active programs as bluish electric impulses flashing through the semiconductors inside the machine suddenly starved of current and dying, one after the other, in electronic dead ends. He turned the computer back on. The CPU clicked, then stopped; the screen remained blank.

7

"You haven't seen Charles, have you?"

Andreas looked up from the desk and put his penknife away.

"Don't get uptight, man. What's with you? You aren't going to get weird on us just because of a stupid math test, are you?"

"Cut it out. This isn't funny. This is really, really serious. I crashed my brother's computer."

"Crashed, as in crash-crashed?"

Eric nodded. Andreas fell silent, impressed by the tragedy.

"I have to find Charles before Gilles gets home. Otherwise, he's going to kill me."

"I thought your brother was in the army."

"He's home on leave."

"Sorry about that, man. Really sorry."

The eight o'clock bell rang. Eric sat down and raked his fingers through his hair. He was bathed in a clammy, unhealthy sweat, which he could feel oozing from his armpits down along his ribs.

Gradually the class filled up, but Charles still didn't appear. Andreas kept glancing at his watch, and Eric realized that this was the very first time since the beginning of the year that his classmate was not only on time, but actually early. Andreas was always coming to school late, and the ingenuity of his excuses had made him famous among his peers. Some of his teachers — though convinced he was one of the biggest dunces they had met in their entire career — even felt a grudging admiration for him on that score.

The math teacher was just getting to his feet to close the door when Charles and Elena walked in. Eric's heart leaped at the sight of her. It was like a dream. He heard the teacher gently rebuke the two latecomers. Then, as if in slow motion, he saw Elena pass Charles, turn into Eric's row, walk toward him, and finally stop to ask, "Is this seat free?"

He nodded without answering, his mouth dry, and slid along the bench to make room for her. Charles sat down next to Andreas.

Elena opened her book bag, pulled out her pencil box and a pad of paper, and smiled at him. Eric was tongue-tied. I'm sweating! he suddenly thought. I'm sweating like a pig, and she's going to smell it! He pulled his elbows against his body to hide the stains under his armpits, where he could feel the cold sweat plastering his shirt to his skin.

"I hope you had a nice trip," said Mr. Maffioli, the teacher. "And that you took advantage of the long weekend to go over the formulas I asked you to learn."

He pulled a folder out of his briefcase and handed a stack of test papers to the first rows, to be passed back. Groans rose, as row by row, the students grasped the dimensions of the test problem. Eric shot a glance sideways. Andreas's eyes were fixed on his watch, and he seemed unconcerned by the drama unfolding around him.

When the test papers finally reached their row, Eric grabbed them and gave one to Elena. She took time to thank him with a smile before starting to read it. Eric had turned around to pass the remaining copies to his neighbors when the explosion went off. Startled, he dropped the papers, which scattered to the floor. Screams filled the room, and some of the students instinctively ducked. Around him, Eric could see looks of fear and growing panic.

"What the hell…" said the math teacher, as a second explosion went off at the back of the class.

The blast's impact blew open the closet door, and thick white smoke blanketed the last rows of desks.

"Evacuate the classroom," shouted Mr. Maffioli. "Everybody out!"

That was a waste of breath. Most of the students were already rushing through the door.

*   *   *

"But how did you do it?"

"That's *my* little secret," Andreas answered, walking faster.

Charles caught up with him and insisted.

"Listen. I'll only tell because it's you, dude. And because you'd never have the guts to try it yourself," he added, winking at Eric.

They were striding along the park, which was still deserted at that hour. It was cold. The sun was rising slowly, burning off the few strands of fog still snagged on the treetops.

"You need a cigarette — a long one — a big firecracker, a needle, and a sugar cube."

"Why a sugar cube?"

"Don't keep interrupting me, geek. With the needle, you dig a hole in the cigarette filter. Then you light the cigarette and slip the end of the firecracker fuse into the filter. Got that?"

"Got it."

"Then you set the whole things down gently in a carefully chosen spot — a closet, say."

"What about the sugar cube?"

"I'm getting to that. You balance the cigarette on the cube with the burning end down and the filter end slightly raised…"

"So the cigarette burns up completely! You're a genius!"

48

"Did you ever doubt it, dwarf?"

"I'm less interested in how than why," broke in Eric. "Why right in the middle of a math test?"

"You poor baby!" burst out Andreas. "And just on the day when your Bosanski sweetheart finally sets her little butt down next to you…"

Andreas made an obscene grimace that left Eric shaken.

"You're out of your mind! That doesn't have anything to do with… What I mean is… what I mean is, we're going to have to take that math test over again anyway. Putting it off doesn't do anything except piss off Maffioli."

"Hey, where's your spirit of adventure?"

Andreas had stopped and held his hand over his heart, looking honestly abashed.

Annoyed, Eric walked on.

"I stayed up all last night to study for that test so I'd get a decent grade, and you screwed everything up."

"You do whatever you like with your evenings, man," Andreas retorted, catching up with Eric. "I spent three hours of mine playing *Doooooommm…*"

"Did you finish level 22?" asked Charles.

"See, the dwarf keeps things straight. He remembers stuff. We could turn him into a grade-A test taker. No, I couldn't finish level 22 because of some goddamned imp… Hey, you know what? You know what I found out? It's so cool, you'll never guess."

Eric shrugged and kept walking.

"The ad campaign for *Doom II*, in England, you know what they did? They filled plastic bags with guts and butcher shop scraps, and sent them to each of the games magazines. Isn't that far out? Can you imagine the secretary at the front desk who gets the package and opens it, and sploosh!…"

Andreas burst into a peal of staccato laughter as he slammed his fist into a lamp pole.

8

"CHECKING... CHECKING..." The words were blinking on Charles's computer screen. Perched awkwardly on the corner of the desk, Eric stared at them, caught between hope and fear. Andreas lay sprawled across the bed, turning the pages of a manual on installing sound cards, without understanding a word of it. Charles's bookcase bulged with technical books on every aspect of computer science. Simple user's guides, like *PC for Dummies*, which Eric and Andreas could master easily, stood next to daunting tech manuals on IRQ conflicts and DMA channels, optimum AUTOEXEC.BAT and CONFIG.SYS settings. Their back-cover blurbs alone would give non-initiates a headache for weeks.

"Ah..." said Charles softly when the screen displayed "Verification complete."

Eric searched his friend's face, hanging on his verdict.

"So, doctor, is it serious?" shot Andreas, without looking up from his reading.

"None of the programs detected any viruses on the diskette."

Eric heaved a sigh of relief.

"That means none of the known viruses, of course. So now we can go to stage two…"

He exited the anti-virus program, logged onto the disk drive, and typed "dir."

The list of files on the diskettes appeared:

INSTALL.EXE

INSTALL.BAT

ULTIMATE.EXE

SETSOUND.EXE

"You said you typed 'install' and didn't get anything, right?" asked Charles.

"I typed 'install,' then 'play,' but nothing happened. So then I tried 'dir' like you just did, and the computer crashed."

"Nothing weird is happening on mine right now. It may be a configuration problem, some conflict between one of the programs and the stuff you have. That happens. Anyway, we'll soon find out…"

Charles made a copy of the diskette, then checked to see that he had everything handy: the cut-off switch, startup disks for his computer, and a backup of the entire contents of his hard drive, which he'd made the night before.

"Synchronize your watches, gentlemen," he muttered, speaking around an imaginary cigar.

He plugged an old external drive into the back of his computer and restarted the CPU.

"If it crashes, or if the program tries to infect the hard disk, all I have to do is erase and reformat it. Let's go…"

Charles typed "A:\install" and the program launched without any apparent hitches. He followed the few instructions, then typed "setsound" to configure the sound card. In a few seconds, the program was installed.

"I don't know what happened with you. Everything's gone just fine. And I'm pretty sure the program isn't infected. You should try again this evening. And if it really crashes, bring it over and I'll fix it here."

Relieved, Eric stood up and started to pull on his windbreaker. If there was no virus, there was no danger that he'd screwed up his brother's hard drive or erased any important data. At worst, he might have to replace a few internal components, and Charles was a whiz at that sort of work. They knew that the high cost of replacing components had more to do with the cost of labor than the price of the actual parts, which was fairly low.

Charles stared at him in amazement.

"You leaving already? Don't you want to see it run?"

"I don't want anything to with that program, not right now. Besides, it's probably a piece of crap."

Andreas had risen up on one elbow. Now he poked Charles's back.

"Hey, let him go if he isn't interested. Let's us have a look. Go ahead: hit it!"

Charles typed "ultimate."

The computer whirred. Greenish lights on the front of the CPU blinked. The screen brightened. Clouds of smoke danced before their eyes. Dull, hypnotic music, in which a muffled drum mixed with a bugle call, filled the room.

"From the very beginnings of time…" The words were French, delivered in a dark, resonant, compelling voice.

"This game's in *French?*" asked Andreas.

Eric and Charles exchanged a puzzled look. Nothing in the installation program showed any choice of language other than English. How did the program know to…? They didn't have the time to ponder the matter. The rich, full voice had resumed: "From the very beginnings of time, the human race has taken part in a game that is the most exciting, most dangerous, and most prestigious game in the universe."

The screen brightened further. The point of view changed, and the boys now had the impression that they were flying rapidly above the surface of a planet, at the very edge of the stratosphere. Wisps of cloud drifted across their field of vision. The illusion of depth was extraordinary. Enthralled, they stared at the screen. The camera plunged downward. The image became more detailed, and Eric sat back, dizzy with astonishment. The clash of weapons reached their ears even before they glimpsed the battlefield: the metallic clang of swords against shields, the low whistle of arrows hitting their targets. For a moment longer, they were still in the clouds, above a hill. Then, in the foreground, a man fell. A Roman soldier, to judge by his uniform. Arrows pierced the screen, seeming to fly straight at them.

Andreas swore softly, so perfect was the illusion. The camera moved on, and they were now in the heart of the fighting, a pitched battle where swords flashed and dead bodies fell like rain. The music became louder and the sound of swordplay was now joined by the rattle of muskets, then the roar of cannons. The camera continued moving, and through the smoke of explosions and screams of pain and rage, they could now make out other men, other enemies, other fighting armies. Here a crusader ran his sword through an infidel, there a soldier from the Napoleonic wars pitched face forward, shattered by a rifle bullet. Further on, World War I infantrymen raced headlong through a mine field and disappeared one after another in the blasts of explosions.

"This ancient game," the voice resumed, "this fascinating game, is the ultimate game. A game of conquest and suffering, a game of victory and death. Are you brave enough to confront *The Ultimate Experience?*"

The title appeared in fiery letters on a black background. The CPU whirred again.

"Son of a bitch," breathed Andreas.

He was now fully alert and standing right behind Charles, his gaze riveted to the screen.

"I don't understand this." Charles examined the diskette with a worried look.

"What don't you understand?" asked Eric.

"That was an incredible full-action video scene, at least four minutes long. With sound, music, special effects... Did you see how detailed the images were? That's the sort of thing you might see on a CD-ROM, and even then, not very often. So how can all that fit on one diskette? And what program is it in?"

"Choose your playing mode," the voice ordered.

On the screen, three options appeared:

    HAND-TO-HAND

    STRATEGY

    ULTIMATE

"I just don't get it," Charles said. And he switched the computer off.

Andreas let out a yelp of disappointment and jumped up, as if about to hit him.

"It isn't normal," said Charles. "In fact, it isn't even *possible*."

Worried, Eric looked at him. His friend's forehead was wet with sweat.

"You really *are* a cyber-jerk, you know that?" shouted Andreas. He grabbed the diskette and shoved it into his jacket pocket.

"What are you doing?" asked Eric.

"Well, it doesn't interest you, and it's making Charles piss in his pants, so *I'm* taking it. And I mean now."

"Wait," said Eric, "Charles's probably right. First we have to understand how..."

"Don't give me any of that stupid crap! What's there to understand? You two can stay here and talk your heads off. Me, I'm going home to try 'Hand-to-hand' mode."

He drew his hand across his throat, pretending to cut off his head, gave a terrifying shout, and vanished down the hallway. Eric and Charles heard the front door slam.

"I'd better get going, too," Eric finally said.

Charles didn't seem to hear him.

"Well, I'm on my way. See you this afternoon at the track?"

"Uh, yeah, right… at the track."

Once he was alone, Charles switched the computer back on. Only one explanation came to mind. The game's programmer must have used some particularly revolutionary data compression technique to fit all of those image and sound files onto a single diskette. When it installed, the program must have decompressed automatically, and was now occupying uncountable megabytes on his hard disk.

Charles tapped at the keys to bring up his file manager, then located the ULTIMATE subdirectory. He double-clicked on the little yellow icon and the folder opened, revealing its contents: four files, the same ones that Charles had copied from the diskette. INSTALL.EXE and INSTALL.BAT, which contained the game's installation program; SET-SOUND.EXE, which contained the sound files; and ULTIMATE.EXE, which launched the game itself, once it was installed. A line at the bottom of the screen displayed the amount of hard disk space taken up by the game:

"Total 4 file(s) 7.68k"

It was impossible, simply impossible. Even a crude game like *Tetris* or a cheesy eighties arcade game took up at least ten times as much space. Over the years, of course, developers had made enormous progress and refined their calculations in creating new games that were more complicated, but more mathematically elegant and less clunky. But to think the creator of *The Ultimate Experience* had managed to make so much fit in so little space… If that were true, then the guy deserved to be in the pantheon of computer science giants, publishing millions of copies of games that would raise him to the rank of a god, and not wasting his time with some back-alley publishing house. The *Doom* programmers were four bearded hippies who started out in a California garage. Now they were all millionaires, competing to see which one could buy the most race cars. At last count, it was three Ferrari Testarossas each, at $200,000 apiece.

Charles had to know for sure. He clicked on SETSOUND.EXE to select the sound file, dragged it to the File menu and chose "Delete." With a last-ditch spasm of regret, the program asked:

"Current directory: C:\Ultimate\SETSOUND.EXE. Delete all?"

Charles chose "Yes" while watching the line at the bottom of the screen. After a few seconds, it read:

"Total 3 file(s) 5.21k"

He repeated the operation with INSTALL.BAT. Now 2.15k remained. At last, he deleted INSTALL.EXE. Then he remained motionless in front of the screen for a long time, trying to grasp the incomprehensible.

The computer now displayed the contents of the last folder in the directory, the ULTIMATE.EXE file.

"Total 1 file(s) 0 k"

The game didn't exist. The program didn't exist. Charles moved the cursor to the file to delete it. His hand was shaking. He was about to click on the file when the screen went black. First he heard the crackle of flames, then the hoarse, impatient voice, ordering: "Choose your playing mode."

9

WHEN ERIC WALKED into his bedroom, Gilles was sitting at the computer, typing.

"Hi, there. Aren't you supposed to be in school?"

Eric was startled for a moment, then relieved.

"No. There was a fire alarm. Classes won't start again until this afternoon."

"A fire alarm?" repeated Gilles, raising his eyebrows.

"Nothing serious... You didn't... you didn't have any trouble starting the computer, did you?" asked Eric, changing the subject.

"No, none. Why? Should I have?"

"No, no, of course not..."

"I even installed your new game, the one over there. You bring it back from England?"

For an instant, Eric thought his brother was talking about *The Ultimate Experience.* But Gilles swiveled around on the chair, picked up the *Fade to Black* manual, and tossed it to his brother.

"It isn't bad at all. Naturally, the processor isn't powerful enough to render the graphics in Super-VGA, but it's still very, very good... And it's a nice change from those blood-and-gore slasher sagas..."

Eric didn't know what to say. He glanced at the

screen and read a few lines at random: "…and dis-gust at myself. I had thought, for once, that I would be useful for something, or someone. To let my actions fit my thoughts. But that didn't take into account the fundamental ambiguity of our mission. I had wanted to be a soldier for peace. An ambitious plan and a fatal error. How many people died?"

Gilles noticed what his brother was up to, and saved and closed the file. The text disappeared. The two brothers sized each other up, exchanged grins.

"I'm happy…

"It's so good to…"

They had spoken at the same time.

"Let's run that one by again," said Gilles, and clapped his hands, mimicking the sound of a movie slate. "'The Older Brother's Return.' Scene forty-six, take two."

"I'm glad you came home in one piece," said Eric.

Gilles's smile faded and his eyes became trou-bled.

"What did you think would happen?"

Eric hesitated.

"Mom and I used to watch the news on TV every night, to see where the fighting was hottest. And with your letters, we followed your moves on a map…"

"A map? Where did you ever find a map of Yugoslavia?"

"At school. The history teacher put it up. And it's a real map from over there, not one printed in France. There's a girl in our class... a Yugoslavian refugee..."

"A refugee..."

"Elena... Elena something," said Eric, shrugging his shoulders to hide his emotion.

"When did she come to France?"

"I don't know. I've never spoken to her. Well, almost never."

"Why not?"

Eric blew out a puff of air to show the subject no longer interested him.

"Does she make you nervous?"

"Screw you!" snapped Eric. He took off his jacket, tossed it on the bed, and stretched out.

"I'd like to meet this girl," Gilles said at last.

"What for?"

"To talk, to find out how she got to France... Is her family with her?"

"Jesus, the questions you ask! How should I know?"

"Don't argue, darlings." Their mother's breathless voice reached them from the shadowy depths of her room.

63

"How is she?" murmured Gilles.

"Not too bad. Munier came to see her last week and ordered her to go out at least every other day."

"And did she?"

Eric shook his head.

10

ON HIS THIRD LAP around the track, Eric joined Charles and Andreas, who were hiding behind the sand pile. One of his classmates shot him a friendly insult and kept on running. It would never occur to anyone to snitch on him to the gym teacher. In any case, the day was cold and Mr. Lorrain had joined his colleagues in the track's warming huts. He wouldn't come out for a good half-hour.

From time to time, one of the phys. ed. teachers would leave the relative comfort of the locker room and appear in the doorway to urge their students on. In the boys' opinion, it was grossly unfair. But at least it allowed them to hide out for a couple of laps, in small groups, behind the sand pile of the long-jump track at the far end of the oval.

"You guys better get going again," said Eric, as he caught his breath. "Otherwise Lorrain might notice you're missing."

"Who gives a shit?" Andreas cut in. "Listen, I take back everything I said about that old guy in England. May Lucifer bless him. May his favorite soccer team win all next year's matches! May his tax collector get crushed by a tractor-trailer truck."

"What are you talking about?"

"Haven't you tried *The Ultimate Experience?*" asked Charles, his eyes shining. "Couldn't you get your computer working again?"

"Yes, but no… I mean the thing's running, but I haven't tried the game again. Especially since I didn't make a copy of the diskette."

"You have to see it with your own eyes," Charles continued. "It's absolutely fabulous. I've never seen anything like it. I spent two hours playing it after you left. If my mother hadn't made me go, I think I'd have cut gym. It's so complex, and so well designed…"

"It's the most mind-blowing game I've ever seen, man. You really feel like you're there. Nothing like the usual 3-D games," added Andreas.

"We were just talking about it when you showed up," said Charles, "and we can't agree on anything. It's as if we didn't play the same game. Andreas picked 'Hand-to-hand' mode, and I started a campaign in 'Strategy.' He chose 'Vietnam War,' and I took 'Verdun.' But nothing we saw onscreen was the same."

"I spent an hour in the rice paddies, slogging through mud up to my knees. There's flames and explosions everywhere. It was so fucking great… "

"I'm commanding a couple of French battalions during a counter-attack at Verdun in November

1916," said Charles. "It's all there. You can check on everything from the weather to how exhausted the troops are—all the stats you could ever want. The game's incredibly detailed. And yet it plays so smoothly..."

"Finally, I found the entrance to a Viet Cong hooch camouflaged under a thick layer of dirt and branches," said Andreas. "I tossed in a couple of incendiary grenades, then finished them off with my knife. It's something I'll never forget..."

"I don't understand what you're talking about," said Eric. "You can't tell me those different levels are all on the same diskette..."

"Skip it," said Charles. "That's not the point..."

"But you said yourself—"

Andreas squeezed Eric's arm, silencing him in mid-sentence.

"Shut up. That's a word of friendly advice. Shut up. If this is a dream, I don't feel like having you wake me up, get it? This game is paradise, man. It's better than booze, better than a woman, better than *Doom*, if you really want to know... You try it, then you can talk."

Andreas stood up and brushed off the damp sand clinging to the hairs on his legs.

"Come on, dude. Two more laps and we go home. I don't want to waste any more time here."

"Me neither," said Charles. "I'm not kidding. Try it. I brought you back the diskette I copied this afternoon. You really have to see this..."

They started running again, leaving a baffled Eric behind the sand pile.

11

"I NEED TO talk to you, Andreas."

"Not now," Andreas muttered between his teeth, without looking at his father.

He was staring at the screen, expecting at any second to see an enemy face appear among the tangle of vines and branches he had been silently hacking through for the last hour.

There was a click as Mr. Salaun's foot pressed the switch on the power strip. The image disappeared as the computer's CPU went dead. Stunned, Andreas looked at the darkened screen for a moment, then exploded.

"Are you out of your mind, or what? D'you have any idea what you just did?"

"I want to talk to you," his father said again. Taking no notice of Andreas's anger, he sat down on the only stool in the room. "The principal phoned your mother this afternoon."

"So what?"

"Your math class was interrupted this morning. In fact, as I understand it, all the classes were interrupted for two hours because of a bomb scare."

"So what?"

"Stop repeating 'So what?'! An ingenious little

device was found in a closet in your classroom. The principal knows you're behind it."

"What d'you mean, he knows?"

"Let's say he has strong suspicions. You shouldn't be surprised."

"Whatever. But to nail me, he'll need proof…"

"That's right. In fact, that's the only reason you didn't get kicked out of school. And that's the point I made in my letter to him."

"Anyway, he's been on my case for years. Every time, it's the same old thing…"

"All the more reason to be careful. I know it was you. And I'm warning you, I don't want any more incidents like this one. Understand?"

"Hey, what's going on here? You're caving in because of the principal, is that it? You're the one who's always saying those people are all scum; that they're niggers, faggots, welfare queens, and camel-jockeys. But I set off one tiny little firecracker, and you…"

The slap caught Andreas across the face and sent him sprawling onto the bed. His father was standing, ready to hit him if Andreas so much as moved. This wasn't the first time they had come to blows, and Andreas knew that in spite of his strength and size, he wouldn't win.

"Discipline, that's all I ask of you," said his father.

"Discipline. You have the right to be angry. You have the right to hate them. You even have the right to hate me. But you must show discipline. It's the only way to triumph over... those people. The time hasn't yet come to meet them head on, and for the moment we still have to keep a low profile."

"So how much longer? Why not right away?"

"Because we aren't ready yet. I forbid you to pull any more stupid stunts at school or anywhere else. You know what responsibilities I have. I don't want some snot-nosed reporter dragging me through the mud because my son is making trouble at his lousy high school."

"You just want respectability, is all."

"Take it any way you like."

"What about your midnight trips into Arab neighborhoods to smash their cars and their stinking mosques? Is that respectable?"

Mr. Salaun grabbed his son by the collar and lifted him off the bed.

"I didn't hear what you just said, you little shit. I erased it from my memory this very instant, and I suggest you do the same."

Andreas nodded, feeling both shame and a delicious sensation of surrender.

"No more screw-ups at school, understand? I don't want you to attract attention."

Mr. Salaun released his son and turned on his heel to go.

"And while you're at it, get rid of the fertilizer and the rest of that crap you have stored in the garage. I don't want your mother to burn the place down when she's parking the car."

12

"GENERAL?"

Charles jumped. The voice sounded so close…
For an instant, he thought someone was next to
him. Even the sound effects were unusual, he
thought, better than the movies, better than Dolby,
better than THX. Even through the computer's tiny
built-in speakers, the sound sometimes seemed to
be coming from right there in the room.

"General?" repeated the voice, as if reluctant to
break into his thoughts.

Moving across the screen was a forest between
Verdun and Montmédy that had been devastated by
artillery fire. A ghostly layer of fog hovered over the
ground. Through it, Charles glimpsed here and
there the shattered remains of a 370-mm mortar or
the limp silhouette of a corpse tangled in strands of
barbed wire.

"General Boisdeffre?" the voice insisted.

Charles turned his head to the right. Captain de
Marigny was looking down at a stack of reports he
had just taken out of his briefcase.

"I'm sorry, general, but we're nearly at the rendezvous. It might help if you looked over some of
the documents that reached us this morning."

Charles was still in shock; he remained slumped on the seat without answering. He cast a dazed look around him. Busy arranging his files, de Marigny didn't seem to notice.

De Marigny must have been nearing fifty, but he was still handsome, and careful about his appearance even in the heaviest fighting. The ends of his mustache, stiff with wax, curved slightly upward, as if to emphasize his vanity.

Just a moment before, Charles had been in his bedroom, trying to repel a concentrated attack on his right flank by the German army. The losses around Verdun had been mounting day by day, and Charles wondered if he hadn't blundered the previous evening, when he'd dismissed General Pétain and entrusted the French counterattack on the western front to General Nivelle.

For several months now, nothing had gone the way he wanted. The high command had sent younger and younger divisions to the front, speeded the rotation of units in the field, reduced, then practically eliminated leave for the soldiers. Yet the German army, which had more men and matériel, had been steadily gaining ground that the French troops weren't able to retake. Without the unhoped-for success of the British offensive on the Somme in June 1916, which had forced the Germans to send several divisions there, temporarily weakening their positions around Verdun, the front would have been overrun long ago.

Nivelle regularly visited his men on the front lines, appealing to the French soldiers' courage and patriotism, telling anyone who would listen, "They will not pass!" But the intensity of the constant bombardment, the frequent disruption of supplies, and the countless casualties were all wearing the troops down.

Charles didn't know the size of the enemy's losses. He figured they must be at least a third of his own, but he didn't have any way to confirm it. What had just happened in May at Laon and Reims suggested that the German troops' morale was no better than the French. Tired of seeing the conflict bogged down for months, Charles had ordered a massive attack along the Aisne front, west of Verdun. Whole French units were sent to assault previously impregnable German strong-points. The front lines had moved several hundred yards forward, but the cost in lives lost had been steep.

None of that would have been catastrophic, because Charles still had the option of drafting into the army conscripts under eighteen years old from the classes of 1916 and 1917. But the risky offensive had had a devastating impact on the soldiers' morale. For several days, combat troops on both sides of the front lines had stopped shooting. Some, carrying white flags, had even crossed into the no man's land separating them, to fraternize.

The situation map now showed that the Aisne front had been static for the past five weeks. As Charles wrestled with this new challenge, a movie-like scene started up on the computer screen. The camera moved along a country road, showing, through the fog, a battlefield several dozen miles long. The dead, bullet-riddled tree trunks, the shell craters full of scummy water, and the monotony of the scene slowly sapped Charles's concentration. His mind wandered and he started to doze off…

I must be dreaming, he told himself. I must have fallen fast asleep in my chair in front of the screen… He knew it would take only a slight effort to wake up, but the situation was so strange and unreal that he decided to stay with it a moment longer. The driver swerved to avoid a pothole, sending General Boisdeffre sliding against his executive officer. A few sheets of paper fell from de Marigny's lap and Charles leaned forward to pick them up.

"Allow me, general…"

De Marigny bent down and searched under the seat. They were riding in the back of a Panhard Levassor, probably a Paris taxi requisitioned by the

French army. Despite the closed windows, the cold seeped in through every crack, and their breath filled the car with clouds of steam. The sensation was so strong that Charles actually shivered.

"General, I was saying that we'll be at the rendezvous in ten minutes or so at most. You just have time to sign these few documents before giving them to General Nivelle."

"Of course, of course," stammered Charles. The sound of his own voice, a middle-aged voice, hoarse and phlegmy, unnerved him.

He glanced at the rear-view mirror in the car, and saw his face, the heavy, lined face of a sixty-year-old man. Petrified, Charles didn't react when de Marigny handed him the documents, just laid them on his knees without reading them. It wasn't just any face; it was really his own, the face he would have a half-century from now. A face in which he recognized some of his father's and grandfather's features. That sight, more than all the rest, unleashed in him a terrible foreboding, the feeling that something uncanny and terrifying was going on. He knew then, without being able to explain how he was so certain, that he hadn't fallen asleep at the computer, that this was no dream. It was spring, the anguished spring of May 1917, and Charles had crossed to the other side of the screen, into the ultimate experience.

13

"Good morning, ladies and gentlemen."

"Good morning," a few voices answered uneasily.

Mr. Maffioli was looking grim. He had walked into the classroom without a word, then waited for the bell to ring, lost in contemplation of a stack of papers on his desk. Eric tried to catch Charles's eye, but his friend was sitting two rows away, on Elena's right, and was staring out at the sky with a strange intensity. Eric turned to follow his gaze, but saw only the clouds slowly drifting by. He shot Elena a questioning look, and she gave him a small, worried smile.

"Because of an incident beyond our control…" the mathematics teacher let his voice linger on the last syllable, searched out Andreas in the room and held his eye for a few seconds, "the math test had to be put off a day. That was too bad, and I'm sure you were as bitterly disappointed as I was. If you weren't, then you will be, starting right now. Because in order to make up the two hours we lost yesterday, and because the school break is coming up soon, today's class will run until 5:30."

"That's unfair," called out a voice from the back

of the class, and Mr. Maffioli wheeled toward it, smiling with feigned sympathy.

"You're absolutely right. It's unfair. And when you see the subject of the test I've created for you today, you'll find it even *more* unfair. In fact, if you weren't going to be glued to your seats for the next two hours, I'm sure you might even send a students-in-distress SOS. You could appeal to the authorities, to the United Nations, or to Doctors Without Borders. But you're out of luck. Thanks to one of your nasty little classmates, you're going to be stuck here past their closing times, wrestling with three especially thorny equations in two unknowns."

"It wasn't our fault," said a girl in the first row. Mr. Maffioli spun around as if he hadn't heard right.

He was clearly relishing this perverse little game. Remembering the panicky expression that had swept across Maffioli's face yesterday, it occurred to Eric that the teacher wasn't about to forgive them for making him look ridiculous.

"It isn't *your* fault, my dear child? I agree. But it's *someone's* fault. And unless the guilty party owns up, or one of you gives me a clue…"

The class held its breath. A few made faces behind the barrier of their closed fists. A very young girl who was one of the best students in the class made an obscene gesture at the teacher from under her desk.

In the silence, the sudden scraping of a chair set their teeth on edge. Eric turned around. All eyes were directed toward the radiator, next to which Andreas had risen and was standing very straight, with a determined look on his face.

"Well, well…" muttered Mr. Maffioli. "I never would have thought…"

Eric frowned and tried to catch Andreas's eye, to stop him. What difference did one math test more or less make? Andreas might get another warning, maybe even get kicked out…

"I have to speak up," Andreas said in a dull voice. "I can't keep this to myself any longer."

"We're listening," said Mr. Maffioli, caught between doubt and triumph.

"It was… it was done by Islamic terrorists. Just before the explosion yesterday, I caught a distinct whiff of couscous."

The class was silent for a moment, then a few laughs broke out here and there. Unable to keep from smiling, Andreas took his seat. Enraged, Maffioli marched to his desk and, jaw clenched, started handing out the tests. He had reached the third row when Charles leaped from his seat with a strangled cry, stretched his arm out toward the blackboard, and collapsed.

* * *

The emergency room hallway was cluttered with empty gurneys. Picking their way among them, Eric and Elena followed the nurse into a white-tiled examining room. Above the head of the bed, a half-dozen electric wires and opaque plastic tubes linked Charles to a battery of monitors. Eyes locked onto his friend's ashen face, Eric didn't hear what the intern on duty was asking. Elena touched his shoulder, and he turned to face the young doctor with a shiver.

"Do you know him? Charles Boisdeffre, right? Do you know him?"

Eric nodded.

"He's a classmate of yours, isn't he? Has he ever had an attack like this before?"

"No, never. Or at least he never mentioned one."

"Do you know if he's under a doctor's care?"

"Beg your pardon?"

"A doctor… Does he have a doctor, a family doctor?"

"Yes, Dr. Munier, same as mine."

"Munier… Munier… He's on Rue de l'Abbaye, isn't he? Could you call him, Beatrice?"

The nurse obeyed, tapping at the wall phone and asking for the operator.

"Now, your friend Charles, does he ever smoke?"

"Oh, no! He hates cigarettes. They make him cough!"

"No, I mean… You know, smoke — a little joint once in a while?"

The intern gave him a conspiratorial smile that Eric for some reason found obscene.

"Oh, no. Especially not Charles. He's completely straight. You've got to be joking. My pal Andreas calls him Mister Clean, so you can imagine…"

"Ah, I see…"

The intern pursed his lips, visibly disappointed by the answer.

"So you don't smoke anything? No liquor either, or drugs?"

"Well, no. Like I said, we're straight."

The intern glanced at Elena and gave Eric an appreciative smile. "Okay, I can see that… What else can you tell me about your pal? Does he do sports? Does he get short of breath? Anything else? Tell me a bit about him."

"No, he isn't into sports. His thing is more electronics. Charles is the one who fixes our computers when we have a problem."

The intern's gaze suddenly brightened.

"A computer? Your friend here has a computer? Does he play video games?"

"Well, sure. Everybody does."

"How much time does he spend in front of his monitor every day?"

"No idea. I've never asked him."

"What about you?"

"One or two hours, sometimes three…"

"You're nuts! Don't you know that's dangerous? You can ruin your eyes with those things, not to mention have epileptic fits!"

Eric was about to answer that his mother soaked up twelve hours of nonstop television every day without apparent ill effects, but changed his mind. He wasn't sure the example was particularly apt.

The nurse interrupted. "I have the treating physician on the line."

As the intern stepped to the phone, Eric and Elena approached the hospital bed, their faces somber. As if by reflex, Charles swallowed and ran a tongue over his dry lips. Behind him, Eric could hear the intern announce to Dr. Munier, in a slightly condescending tone, that he had diagnosed young Boisdeffre as having had an epileptic fit. This must have surprised Munier, because the intern continued with a touch of self-importance:

"What can I say? Sometimes you just have to ask the right questions. He spends nearly three hours a day in front of his computer screen…"

Eric was about to turn around to interrupt the conversation, to object, but Charles's eyes were boring into his.

"The game…"

Those were the first words Charles had spoken since the attack. He hadn't said a thing while lying on the ground with his eyes rolled back in his head, or later, in the ambulance.

Eric nodded, to show he'd heard.

"Don't play it. Whatever you do, don't play it. You understand me?"

Eric was dumbfounded, but he nodded again. Elena was following their conversation closely.

"Tell Andreas… Tell Andreas he has to stop… He doesn't realize…" murmured Charles, closing his eyes.

Eric thought he had fallen asleep, but Charles added: "He doesn't know what he's doing."

14

THE RAIN BEGAN FALLING as Eric and Elena left the hospital grounds. They had started to run when they caught sight of their bus, but it drove off around the corner of the boulevard. The wind rose, and the bus-stop shelter provided them no protection against the blasts of rain that were now soaking them. The two started walking, leaning forward into the wind, hoping against hope that someone would give them a lift. But the cars passed without noticing them, splashing the sidewalk with sheets of muddy water. Drenched and chilled, they walked on. Very gradually, without even noticing it, they moved closer together. Eric took Elena's arm to keep her from stumbling, as he would have taken his mother's arm under similar circumstances.

Gradually the rain let up, and a rainbow even appeared. So far, they hadn't said a word to each other. On the way to the hospital, the presence of the nurse next to Charles had made talking awkward; on the way back, the rain had drowned any attempt at conversation. In any case, Eric didn't know what to say. They were getting close to downtown and their school, but he didn't see how they could go straight back to class, soaked as they were. He didn't even know what time it was. To find out, he would have had to free his arm from Elena's to look at his watch — and that was out of the question.

Walking on, they came to a final fork in the road. Without thinking, Eric turned right, toward his own house and away from the school. He was ready for anything, ready for Elena to resist, to ask him if he wasn't taking the wrong road, maybe even to slap him. But she said nothing, just huddled a little closer. She was shaking. So was he, though he tried to convince himself he had a fever. Just then, his heart jumped to his throat. What would his mother say if she saw him in this state? What would she imagine, seeing Elena? Mortified at the thought, he walked on like a robot. He had to say something, anything, had to turn around and go back. He raised his head, seeking inspiration. Elena's hair, dripping with rain, stuck to her cheek. A few yards ahead of them, he saw Mrs. Boisdeffre parking her car.

It was already five in the afternoon, and dusk was gathering outside. The two of them were alone in the big empty house, and Eric had led Elena into his friend's room. Charles's mother had reacted to the news about her son with a coolness that contrasted with her insisting that they come inside to dry off. Eric was careful to stress that Charles had spoken to them, that he was conscious, that he was not injured. Mrs. Boisdeffre nodded without answering, while vainly tapping at the telephone dial pad.

"I can't seem to reach my husband. Would you mind waiting until he gets home? Tell him I've gone to the hospital. You can both change your clothes; you're soaked."

It was probably too late to go back to class, Eric thought. Besides, the idea of staying alone with Elena in the big house — with a grown-up's blessing — instead of heading for school, struck him as too good to be true.

Eric was sitting on Charles's bed, energetically rubbing his hair with a towel as the sounds of the shower reached him from the bathroom. He had to make an effort to concentrate on what he was doing. His legs, as if powered by internal springs, jiggled uncontrollably against the edge of the bed. Without thinking, he found himself standing next to the bathroom door, his hand on the doorknob, trying to swallow the nervous lump in his throat. He glanced wildly around the too-neat room that he thought he knew so well. Computer magazines were carefully stacked in the bookcase, along with models of fighter planes, Charles's father's waterpolo medals, photographs of first communions and family weddings (the only decoration allowed on the walls): they all seemed to belong to some distant past. Elena's presence in the bathroom had drastically changed the place, lending it an aura of mystery and danger. But before he could make a move, the door opened.

"How do you feel?"

Charles turned his head toward the door. He could make out Dr. Munier's face in the half-light and fumbled for the remote control device, but when he pushed one of the buttons, the head of his bed rose about six inches.

"Don't bother, it's over here," said Munier. He pulled a small plastic cord near the night table, and the overhead light came on.

The doctor sat on the edge of the bed, a half-smile on his lips.

"You don't look so good."

"I'm tired... just tired... I feel like sleeping... but I'm okay. Do you know if anyone's told my parents?"

"I can't say. The hospital called me, so I imagine they were able to get hold of your parents. What happened to you?"

"I had a dizzy spell."

"What else?"

"I wasn't feeling well. I wanted to get up to go to the window."

"You couldn't breathe?"

"Yeah… It was as if I had cotton in my ears, and I felt hot and cold at the same time."

"Had you eaten lunch?"

"Well, not really…"

"So when did you last eat?"

"Last night."

"Last night!"

Munier shook his head and thought for a moment. "Did you tell that to the emergency room intern?"

"No, he didn't ask me."

"And tell me, did you hurt yourself when you fell? Did you cut yourself, or bite your tongue?"

"No."

"Have you ever had dizzy spells like this before?"

"Never."

"And did you… did you soil yourself when you fainted?"

"Beg pardon?"

"Did you urinate? Did you piss on yourself?"

"No!"

Mrs. Boisdeffre burst into the room like a tornado. She met Munier's eye, and, as the doctor rose from the bed with a reassuring smile, rushed over to her son. Trying to control her anxiety, she listened distractedly to the doctor's comforting words. Charles saw something in his mother's eyes that he hadn't seen in a long time, and a weight that had been pressing on his chest since the previous day eased a bit.

"I don't think it was an epileptic fit at all," Munier was saying. "From what Charles tells me, it's more likely that he went into shock from hypoglycemia, that's all. He hadn't had a thing to eat since the previous evening. It's not surprising he fainted."

"But the emergency room doctor told me it probably had something to do with his computer, with the games he plays on it…"

"Frankly, I don't think there's any connection. You know, many of my patients spend several hours a day in front of their TV screens and they don't have *grand mal* seizures every five minutes."

"Anyway, it's over," Charles broke in, from the depths of his bed.

His voice was firm, in marked contrast to his pallor. The two adults turned to him in surprise.

"It's over. I'm never going to touch that computer again."

15

ELENA'S LONG HAIR was still damp. She pulled it back and looked for a place to leave her towel. Coming out of the bathroom, she had found herself face-to-face with Eric. Just for a moment, their breaths mingled. He had a tangy smell, the smell of a boy's nervousness, and she momentarily wondered what his lips would taste like. Blushing with embarrassment, Eric didn't notice her secret amusement. He stammered something about the rain and about having to dry his hair so as to not catch cold. Elena nodded gravely, straining not to burst out laughing. She knew immediately why he had been standing behind the door. He had heard the water running and pictured her taking a shower, but couldn't get up the nerve to join her. And now, trapped in his lie, Eric was alone in the bathroom, energetically scrubbing his scalp with a towel while it was Elena's turn to wait on the other side of the door.

If only Charles's dad doesn't come home too soon, she thought. That would be a shame. For some weeks now, Elena had noticed how Eric had been acting, with his absent look and his clumsy attempts to approach her, which were so different from those of the boys she was used to. In fact, she

had never gotten used to them... Eric was imma-
ture, much less grown-up than she was, even though
he was only two years younger. But without realizing it, he was stirring memories in her, memories
from before the war of another world where everything was clearer, brighter, sweeter. And then her
country had gone insane. Caught up in the hysteria,
she had wanted to grow up too fast, eager to experience the pleasures of sex before it was too late. Her
hurried initiation and the two years of lies and de-
ceptions that followed had left her with a bitter taste.

Her first lover was a friend of her father's who
had quickly disappointed her. A rich wine mer-
chant, Mihail had held out the promise of a glitter-
ing future, only to ditch her with a check and a gold
watch when she thought she might be pregnant.
She wasn't, but the lesson had been a painful one.
She'd had two lovers after that, but one of them, a
political dissident named Stefan, had been arrested
in a raid for publishing a banned satirical newspaper. Elena herself had been interrogated for a long
time, until her father used his connections to get her
released. Soon afterward, he packed her off to stay
with her aunt, who was married to a French engi-
neer. His pretext was that times were hard and that
she risked being corrupted by what he called "ban-
dits and hooligans." Elena was mortified, but had to

swallow her resentment. If her father only knew that Stefan wasn't the first man she had slept with, that one of his best friends, a man he went hunting with every weekend, had already stolen his daughter...

Elena said nothing, accepted the punishment — and began to get to know France, first with surprise, then with joy. She felt at ease here, far from the fighting and the warlike speeches. To improve her French, she had made herself regularly watch the news on television. Maps of her country would appear on the screen daily, accompanied by reports that she had trouble understanding and images of bored soldiers standing around in the snow. Occasionally, politicians from her country were interviewed, and she would turn up the volume to try to catch the rhythm of her native tongue beneath the voice-over translation. But most of them spoke in French or English anyway, probably to show off their education. The exceptions were some of the military people, plain-spoken men who seemed contemptuous of the way the others played up to the West. Some she recognized, decorated heroes whose prowess she remembered being praised on the radio at home. But Stefan, who called himself an anarchist, despised them. Elena didn't share his ideas, but she loved that rebellious side of him.

As her grasp of French improved, she gradually

discovered that Stefan's opinions were more widespread than she had thought. Most French journalists — misinformed, no doubt — were practically calling these great generals "killers" and "war criminals." When she realized this, she felt betrayed and rejected by a country she was starting to love. "War criminals!" Easy for the French to say! And how inappropriate coming from a nation that proclaimed the rights of man while dealing in arms! As if every war didn't carry within it the seeds of crime... What gave Westerners the right to label people, calling some refugees and others aggressors, some victims and others executioners? War was horrible, Elena knew that. But the French reporters seemed to forget that it was sometimes a necessary horror.

Elena folded her towel and laid it on Charles's desk. Her hand brushed the keyboard of his computer, and the screen saver of colorful fishes swimming in blackness vanished, replaced by a scene of a ruined village. Startled, she hesitated for a moment. The image looked exactly like a picture on television. She grasped the mouse on the desk and moved it; the cursor made a small circle on the screen. From the bathroom, she could hear Eric coughing to cover the sound of the toilet flushing. Onscreen, the field of view narrowed as the computer zoomed in on a street corner. Elena now found herself looking down at the scene, as if she were in a helicopter. She could make out three men in fatigue pants and camouflage jackets. The image was so detailed that she could distinguish little puffs of steam coming from their mouths. They were in a triangle, walking casually, their weapons pointed outward. She put the cursor on one of the men and clicked the mouse. A series of statistics appeared in a bar at the bottom of the screen, then disappeared when she lifted her finger. Caught up in the game, she moved the cursor to the entrance of a dilapidated building — an inn, its roof caved in by shelling. The character she had initially clicked on now changed direction and headed for the wooden door, followed by his comrades. A few clouds passed overhead, creating fleeting shadows at their feet. Then everything happened very fast. An old woman came out of the inn, sputtering insults. The closest man waved the barrel of his weapon at her and yelled at her to be quiet. Her answer was to spit in his face.

Elena's finger tightened on the mouse. A burst of gunfire cut the old woman down and sent her tumbling backwards, her arms and legs twitching in an obscene jig. Then she collapsed, leaving a long reddish stain on the rough-textured wall.

In shock, Elena dropped the mouse, frowning as

if to keep from seeing what was happening on-screen. Far away, very far away, a telephone was ringing. The three men walked into the inn, and the roof magically vanished to reveal the entire ground floor, as if they had stepped into a cut-away doll's house. They moved forward calmly and methodically, careful not to get into each other's line of fire, taking turns covering the point man. Something about their skill awoke a deep feeling of panic in Elena, though she couldn't have said why. They walked between the tables, and one of them went behind the bar. The cursor moved to a trapdoor hidden under a pile of empty cardboard boxes. The point man stepped forward, kicked the boxes aside, and raised the trapdoor. In the light you could see the top rungs of a ladder against damp cellar walls. Shouts rang out, women started crying and children wailing.

"Zoran!" shouted the point man. "This one's for you."

He had spoken in Serbian, Elena's mother tongue. Zoran ran up, fumbled in his backpack, pulled out a shiny black object. A long scream now rose from the cellar, becoming an unbearable, almost inhuman shriek. Elena put her hands over her ears, tried unsuccessfully to close her eyes. Zoran pulled the pin on the grenade, tossed it down the hatch, and quickly drew back, followed by the point man. They had reached the end of the bar when a woman burst out of the opening, carrying a child at arm's length. The man fired without bothering to take aim. A muffled explosion rocked the cellar, briefly illuminating the woman and the child in a holocaust of flame. Bodies ablaze, they fell back into the darkness.

The camera angle changed, dropping down level with the three men's faces. The third man took a pack of Lucky Strikes from his flak jacket and held the cigarettes out to the others before taking one.

"Nice hunting, Zoran. You're buying the drinks tonight."

The point man let out a savage, satisfied laugh. Elena's father, taking a drag on his cigarette, merely shrugged.

16

DOWNSTAIRS, the front door slammed. Eric rushed out of the bathroom, feeling vaguely guilty. That must be Charles's dad, he thought. He didn't want a grown-up to catch him like this, his hair messy and his cheeks hot.

To his amazement, Charles's room was empty. Elena's towel was lying the floor. He walked along the hallway and down the first steps of the big staircase leading to the ground floor. Nobody was there. Only then did Eric realize she had left, had fled. Torn between disappointment and a kind of relief, he returned to the bedroom and looked around, as if it might hold some sort of clue. He picked up the towel and raised it to his face. It smelled of soap mixed with something else, something more intimate that made his head spin. He stopped breathing for a few moments, drunk on the fragrance. He wondered what time it was. Outside, night had fallen. He considered phoning home to reassure his mother, but decided against it. Mrs. Boisdeffre had given him a mission and he would carry it out to the end. The circumstances of Charles's attack, the trip in the ambulance, returning in the rain with Elena — it all felt like part of a dream.

Eric sat down at the computer and tapped at the keyboard. The words "Connection established" blinked onscreen.

A map appeared on the right-hand part of the screen, a map of a village surrounded by hills. A bar at the left gave information on the village's productive capacity and the number of its inhabitants. A clock face at the top of the screen ticked off the minutes; in the game, it was 4:22 P.M. Eric slid the cursor over to the map, and the screen displayed the characteristics of each building in turn.

"Santa Maria Church. Resistance: 450 points. Capacity: 1,226 people. Production: 0.

"Weapons factory. Resistance: 125 points. Capacity: 135 people. Production: 145.

"City Hall. Resistance: 175 points. Capacity: 225 people. Production: 0. Arms and ammunition: 192."

Intrigued, Eric clicked on the city hall, which grew to fill the entire right side of the screen. By trial and error, he figured out how to review the village's resources and query the computer. "Enemy resources?" he typed. "Unknown," it replied. "Object of the current mission?" he asked. "Defend the village," he was told. "Game playing mode?" he finally asked. On the keyboard, his fingers were trembling. He remembered Charles's warning, but the excitement of the last hours had been so intense — and the memory of Elena's closeness so present in his mind — that playing the game was less a pleasure than a way of curbing his frustration.

The words "Multiplayer mode" appeared. Eric jerked upright in his chair, and left the game for a moment to examine the computer in front of him. He knew Charles was a master at jury-rigging things, that he loved nothing better than taking apart and reassembling his PC, adding a memory chip there, creating a hard-disk cache there. But he had never said anything about getting a modem. Eric walked around the desk to inspect the back of the CPU. The cables, which on his and Andreas's computers were snarled in dusty tangles, were here carefully labeled and housed in protective sheaths. Eric examined them one after another, but found nothing out of the ordinary. There was no modem to be seen, either on the desk or in the drawers. Charles could have installed an internal fax modem card of course, but there would still have to be a connection between the CPU and the phone line. Eric picked up the telephone, and followed the line to the phone jack. There were no connections, no junctions, nothing.

He sat back down at the screen. In the distance, he seemed to hear a rumbling sound. Feverishly, he typed: "Identify opponent." "Fragmeister," answered the machine. "Code name: Condor." The next line scrolled onscreen: "So, dude, out of the hospital already? Watch out, I'm sending you right back there!"

Sweat appeared on Eric's forehead. He typed:

"This is Eric. I'm at Charles's place. What's happening?"

"What's happening? What's happening is I'm going to cut you to ribbons, babycakes."

"I'm serious, Andreas. How are we connected?"

"The Holy Ghost did it, man. What the fuck do I care? Are you here to play or to talk? This isn't a tits-and-ass phone-sex line, man!"

"Andreas, quit it. Charles said to stop. We absolutely must talk first."

"You're a drag and a half. You playing or surrendering?"

"Do you have a modem? What's connecting us?"

"The game, numb-nuts. We're connected by the game. In case you haven't noticed, that's the only thing that connects us."

"We have to stop, Andreas. We have to talk this over."

"The game has already started, you asshole. I can't go back. You have two minutes to make up your mind. Position your defenses or declare forfeit. Over and out."

The rumbling had grown louder. Eric found himself back at the startup screen with the map. For a moment, he felt like letting it all drop and switching off the monitor. But Andreas's nastiness had stung him, so he decided to fight.

Eric clicked on the city hall, selected his troops, and sent them out along the town's main access routes. Then he feverishly built road-blocks, taking advantage of any available natural features: a bridge here, an empty barn near a cornfield there. Within the village, he deployed the men who were the best shots high in the church bell tower and on the roofs of the city hall, the school, and the farmers cooperative. Looking the situation over in a moment of respite, he wondered what Charles would do in his place. Eric knew that he didn't think strategically, the way Charles did. What eventualities had he overlooked? He gathered the civilians — the old people, women, and children — in the center of the village near the church, where they could take shelter in an emergency, if his opponent managed to overrun one of his defenses. The enemy forces were now very close. On the alert, Eric tried to determine their position. He expected to see a column of tanks or military trucks come rumbling down from the hills any moment now. He controlled his trembling and ran his tongue over dry lips.

As the roaring became even louder, Eric realized it was coming from the east. He clicked on the troops to the west of town and pointed them towards the two possible enemy entry points. His units got underway, but too slowly for Eric's taste. They were hampered by the civilians walking around the town's main square. I should have stuck them in the church, he thought. They aren't doing me any good, and now they're in the way. His reinforcements were finally reaching the eastern entrances to the village when the first line of bombers appeared on the horizon, just above the mountains.

17

"ELENA! ELENA! Your father's on the phone!"

Her aunt Marianne's well-modulated voice chilled her. Curled up in bed, surrounded by fashion magazines that she had been riffling through without seeing for the last hour, Elena froze — silent, motionless, absent.

She could hear footsteps on the stairs. Feeling trapped, she waited for her aunt to appear in the doorway.

"What's the matter, darling?" she asked. "Didn't you hear me? Your dad's on the line."

Elena took the portable phone that was handed to her, looked at it as if it were an insect, and put it to her ear with distaste.

"Hello, sweetheart. How are you?"

The familiar sound of her native tongue didn't soothe her.

Despite the distance and the phone's static, her father's voice was there, right at hand, ringing with warmth and emotion. She wanted to scream, but instead forced herself to reply, in a monotone, "I'm fine, thanks."

"I can't hear you very well, honey. Talk louder. How is your school work?"

"School's fine."

There was a surprised silence at the other end. Then her father's voice came on, full of solicitude: "What's the matter, baby?"

"Everything's fine."

Her father gave a short laugh. "Come on, little *dragiza*, you know you can't hide anything from me. What's wrong?"

"Nothing. I think I caught a cold. I... I came home from school in the rain."

"Take good care of yourself, darling. Ask your aunt to call a doctor if you don't feel well."

"I'll be all right. It's just a passing thing. What about you? How are you doing?" she asked, to avoid having to answer any more questions.

"Fine, *dragiza*, fine. Business is a bit difficult, but nothing worth worrying about."

"How was your hunting trip?"

"My hunting trip?"

"Sure. You told me you were going hunting in the mountains with Zeljko and Mihail this weekend."

"I don't remember... I mean, I don't remember telling you about it. But yeah... We went hunting... in the mountains."

"Did you shoot any game?"

This was the first time Elena had ever taken an

interest in her father's hunting trips. Before, she had always preferred to ignore them. Sounding very ill at ease, he stammered: "You know, at this time of year there really isn't a lot of…"

"Yeah, I imagine that there isn't much left to hunt. Maybe you should think of giving the game time to reproduce."

"What did you say? I'm having a lot of trouble hearing you."

"Nothing. Don't worry about it. Say hello to Mihail for me."

"I'll be glad to. And you, say hello to your uncle for me. When all this stupid political stuff is done with, I'll come visit you."

"That's wonderful. Your prey will be relieved."

"I beg your pardon?"

She didn't answer.

"Hello, hello?… Elena? Hello?"

Her hand shaking, Elena set the phone on the night table and hung up.

18

THE DEAFENING THUNDER of the bombs had fallen silent. Eric staggered through the ruined alleys, stumbling on rubble and charred, smoking beams. Around him, the town was silent. He could occasionally hear a wall or a roof collapse in the distance. First one brick would come loose, then another, and another, in a rhythmic avalanche. Clouds of dust rose into the sky here and there, blocking the springtime afternoon light. Eric, who had completely lost his bearings, was heading in what he thought was the direction of the town square, guided by a sporadic crackling. At first, he imagined men were firing into the air, in the vain hope of shooting down an enemy fighter plane. Then a dull explosion blew the air out of his lungs and sent him sprawling to the ground, badly scraping his elbows in the process. The crackling grew louder. Eric got to his feet, only to see a wall of flames leaping from one building to the next in the alleyway a dozen yards ahead. Pissing in terror, he spun round and sprinted back the way he had come, trying to escape the inferno.

The Heinkels were buzzing the fields, their

machine guns mowing down the last survivors hiding in the corn. On the computer, the image of the devastated village was replaced by the end-of-level stats. Andreas sat up in his chair, stretching his cramped muscles.

MISSION NUMBER: 4
CONDOR LEGION, April 1937
MISSION TOTAL ELAPSED TIME: 26 minutes 43 seconds
MISSION RESULTS: Objective 86% destroyed
HUMAN LOSSES: 0
MATERIAL LOSSES: 0
ENEMY LOSSES: 1,007 dead, 1,518 wounded
GUERNICA ATTACK: Total success

Andreas tapped on the keyboard. His insignia, a condor clutching a swastika, appeared above the screen where the campaign figures were tallied. The scores flashed onscreen like a pinball machine's.

Fragmeister, code name CONDOR: 32,530 points
Boisdeffre, code name _____?: 1,993 points

"Beaten to a pulp, kiddies. I made mincemeat out of you."

Andreas drummed his fingers on the edge of the

keyboard, and he even stood up to do a little victory dance, but his eyes never left the screen. He was fascinated by the promise revealed by the figures in the campaign tally: 32,530 points! He had beaten the stuffing out of his opponent. But more than that, he could imagine the dimensions of the conquests that still awaited him, the extent of the damage he would yet cause. Andreas did the math in his head, taking care not to drop any figures. Tens of thousands. Hundreds of thousands. Millions… He could cause millions of deaths, if he wanted to. Eager to continue the game, he sat down and tried to contact Eric. But from the other side of the screen, nobody answered.

19

ERIC SPENT THE NIGHT moaning and tossing in his bed. Around 3 A.M., a worried Gilles got up in the darkness and put his hand on his brother's forehead; he was burning with fever.

Eric had come home late the night before, about nine o'clock. He answered his mother and his brother's questions with barely coherent scraps of sentences, claiming he had escorted one of his classmates to the hospital then been caught in a rainstorm. In fact, his clothes were soaked, and when he had taken them off and was sitting on the edge of the bed, Gilles could see bloody scrapes on his brother's elbows and forearms.

"Were you in a fight?" he asked.

Eric stared at his arms, as if surprised, then answered in a shaky voice:

"No. I slipped and fell in the alleyway. I hurt myself falling down."

Eric had gone straight to bed, and Gilles decided not to ask him any more questions. But he was struck by his brother's haggard look and the vagueness of his answers. He waited until Eric was asleep, then looked through his clothes, searching his jacket and pants pockets for some sort of clue. He

found nothing, neither a suspicious pack of cigarettes nor any sign of drugs. But Gilles still thought
his brother's slowness and vacant gaze were signs
that he was stoned on something. He decided to
tackle the problem head-on the next day, but was
reassured during the night when he realized Eric
had a high fever.

Gilles went back to bed after downing a tranquilizer. For the last two months, he had been knocking
himself out with sleeping pills to keep from dreaming, or having to remember his dreams. To avoid
finding himself for the hundredth time on the hill-
side north of Lehovici at the moment when the ex-
cavators were switched off and he and his comrades,
armed with metal probes and shovels, climbed
down into the pits to uncover faded tennis shoes and
bones still wrapped in shreds of clothing. To never
again relive the moment when his hand brushed
aside a clump of earth to uncover a smashed Barbie
doll swathed in rotting adhesive tape.

The phone woke them around nine o'clock.
Gilles picked up the receiver and answered. From
the end of the hallway, he could hear the sound of
the television. Mother was up — in a manner of
speaking.

"Hi, it's me, Andreas. So, Chicken Little, you
feeling better now?"

"This is Gilles. Eric's still sleeping. I think he caught a bad cold."

"Hey, bummer. What about you? How are you?"

"I'm fine, thanks. I was about to get up anyway."

Andreas didn't seem to hear the touch of sarcasm in Gilles's voice and forged ahead.

"Eric told me you came home. That's really cool!"

"I'm just on leave. I have to report back this afternoon."

"Hey, that's too bad, man. I'd have liked to hear about…"

"Hear about what?"

"I dunno, everything… What was it like?"

For a moment, Gilles was silent, caught between shame and a desire to hang up. He had never particularly liked Andreas, but he wished he were able to answer him.

"It isn't something I can explain in two seconds on the telephone…"

"I know, man, but at least you can tell me… Was it violent? Were you afraid?"

"I was afraid at times, yes. I was very bored, and I was afraid."

"Did you shoot anybody?'

"No."

"In six months, you didn't shoot anyone? Wow,

talk about keeping a low profile! Did you see any dead guys?"

"Yes, I saw dead people." Gilles's voice was neutral. He heard himself answering as if someone else were speaking. "I even picked some up and carried them."

Andreas didn't answer. Gilles glanced at his brother. Eric was awake, hair matted on his sweaty forehead, and was listening carefully.

"Any more questions?" asked Gilles.

"Nah. Can I talk to Eric?"

"Here he is."

Eric took the receiver and coughed. Gilles turned around and started stripping the sheets from his cot, listening intently.

"Yeah... No, no way... That's your problem... Charles asked you to stop, he says it's dangerous, so I'd be surprised if he did it again with you... That's your problem... No, once and for all, no! I'm not trying it again... I'm gonna to leave it alone, and I think you should, too... No, Andreas, you're the only who thinks it's funny... So? Do it by yourself then... It's no fun by yourself? Listen, you asshole, you think it was *fun* for me last night? You think it was fun for the people who were *with* me?"

Andreas's nervous laughter echoed in the receiver.

"You're nuts," Eric continued in a loud voice. "You're out of your fucking mind. You have to be a real sicko to think that's funny…" A long silence followed, during which Andreas was probably trying to justify himself. Then: "No… That kind of blackmail won't work… Don't tell me about it. I don't want…" Eric's voice weakened, became hesitant. "Don't do that!"

Gilles spun around, alarmed by his brother's shout. Eric was standing on his bed, deathly pale. For a second, Gilles thought he glimpsed flames on the computer screen. He blinked, but when he looked again, the screen was blank. Eric put the receiver down and ran a hand though his hair.

"Eric, I think we'd better talk…" Gilles began.

He was convinced the situation involved drugs, and that Andreas had dragged Eric and Charles into it. He was prepared for anything, except the question his brother asked:

"What's the story with Guernica?"

20

"GENERAL… The chaplain says they're ready."

Charles opened his eyes, tried to stay calm. The doctors busied themselves around him. He heard the wheels of his gurney squeak as it was pushed aside. Strong hands seized him and set him down on the scanner table. Above him, the IV pouch swayed, reflecting the light from the powerful overhead light bank.

"General…"

The voice was more insistent now, drowning out the reassuring hubbub of the radiology department. Charles was still able to hear a nurse's brief laugh, and had the time to think: "The IV… They must have given me a tranquilizer for the scan… I can't let myself fall asleep…" Then a hand touched his shoulder and brought him back to the present. De Marigny stepped back a few paces to let him get up from the sofa where he had dozed off. Charles nodded to his executive officer to bring him his cape and gloves.

After a brief hesitation, he took the clothes he was handed. He knew in advance everything that would happen next; he had already lived through the scene twice before. The first time while alone, seated in front of his computer, the second right in the middle of the classroom, as the math teacher was handing out the test.

Each time, he had tried to resist. In vain.

Without a word, he let himself be led out to the landing, then downstairs to the inn's ground floor. As he passed, the innkeeper doffed his cap and nodded respectfully. They stepped out into the courtyard, where a gleaming De Dion Bouton awaited them. Charles sat down in the back, cutting off his aide-de-camp's chatter with a weary gesture. The car started up, escorted by a small truck, and drove across devastated battlefields where only a few shattered tree trunks protruded from a sea of mud. Don't do anything, thought Charles. It's just a dream, a nightmare. And the only way to be free of it is probably to stay with it all the way to the end.

The car stopped, as it had the two previous times, at the campaign's general headquarters, a small bunker protected from enemy fire by a hill half a dozen yards high. If Charles remembered right, 3,216 men had died for that hill over the last few months. At the time, he had thought the cost was worth it. Now he wasn't so sure.

He was escorted among groups of officers, shook a few hands, and greeted the new infantry commander, Lieutenant General Philippe Pétain. They exchanged a few words as they walked side-by-side toward the execution site. Charles kept his gaze fixed on the ground. He couldn't meet the eyes of the men who now surrounded them on all sides without trembling. Row upon row, hundreds, thousands of soldiers stood at attention in the mud. The first time he saw them, it had made him dizzy. There were so many that from a distance they no longer looked like individuals at all, but a shapeless mass, a gigantic, motionless grey wave that could crest and break down on the officers at any moment. Of course, they had been allowed to keep their weapons, thought Charles. Respect for authority must be enough to keep them quiet, to make them submit. But there are so many of them and only a handful of us. All it would take would be for one of them to rebel and grab his rifle... He raised his head, forced himself to look at the men. A swirl of contradictory feelings raged behind their impassive faces.

It had all been carefully explained to him, at the highest levels, before he left Paris for the front. The troops were exhausted and needed to feel supported, taken in hand. General Nivelle had had too many failures to be able to remain in command. Pétain, who had been dismissed the year before, still retained among the men the image of a leader, a father who was strict but fair. To re-establish his authority, it was necessary that Boisdeffre — who to most of the troops represented the high command, the government, and the French state in all its splendor — be present during this ceremony of atonement. His presence would reinforce the soldiers' feeling of being at fault and block any second thoughts they might have about what was going to happen in the next few minutes.

They had failed, all of them, along the entire front around Laon. They had laid down their rifles and fraternized with the enemy. They had, according to the language of the report that Charles himself had signed, "refused to obey orders." It had been necessary to bring up fresh troops from the rear and arrest the most determined mutineers before the fighting could resume. But there were too many of them, and their collective fault was too great, to even consider shooting them all. As punishment, it had been decided to draw lots to pick the mutineers who would be executed as an example, and that their own brothers in arms would be the ones to carry out the sentence.

Finally, they got within sight of the firing squad. The sun had been up for barely an hour and the air was still heavy with the night's dampness. Charles shivered. Followed by General Pétain, he stationed himself slightly behind the firing squad. De Marigny nervously pulled out a cigarette case and slowly walked from one condemned man to the next, offering each a cigarette. The silence was complete. From far away came an occasional burst of faint barking, borne on the wind. So there's still an animal alive in this hell, thought Charles. He looked up and scanned the sky. Not a single bird. Not a blackbird, not a titmouse, not even a crow.

"The Lord moves…" murmured a voice by his side.

General Boisdeffre turned in surprise. The chaplain gave him a smile full of wisdom and compassion.

"The Lord moves in mysterious ways…"

Charles's bafflement must have been obvious, because the chaplain went on, as if embarrassed at having to explain what he meant.

"It's a test, of course. A terrible test, for them as it is for us. And for Him, too. But it's the price we pay for our sins."

Just for an instant, Charles was seized by doubt. Could this be a message intended for him? A way of saying that the scene about to unfold represented a punishment for the hours he had spent sending thousands of men to be slaughtered merely to satisfy his love of military strategy?

"What… What do you mean?"

"These men have failed, General. Individually and collectively. By refusing to obey orders, they have endangered not only their division and their corps, but the entire nation. Only through a just punishment can they atone for their sin."

A cold, inhuman anger filled Charles's chest. "Would you mind stepping back a bit?" he heard himself say. "The wind is blowing the smell of bullshit my way."

He turned around and walked up next to the firing squad. De Marigny, his task accomplished, had moved aside. The condemned soldiers' ritual cigarettes were lit. The chaplain gave General Boisdeffre a troubled look, then stepped forward to administer last rites to each of the men.

As on the first two times, Charles was seized by a desire to run away. His left hand rested on the pommel of his saber. In a few seconds, he would draw the sword from its scabbard and point it to the sky. Anything but this, he thought. He closed his eyes and concentrated. It's a test, of course. A terrible test, for them as it is for us… The chaplain's voice was still ringing in his ears. He emptied himself of all feeling, forced himself, as if in a dream, to leave his body behind… Charles opened his eyes and found his head encircled by the scanner's metal frame.

"Please don't move, young man. We're almost finished."

Charles tried to speak, but his mouth felt mushy. He raised an arm to free himself, and felt the sharp sting of the IV on the inside of his elbow.

"He's getting agitated. Increase the Valium."

He heard steps coming closer and a woman murmuring something reassuring. I won't move, thought Charles. No need for anesthetic, I'm not going to…

A deep sleep gripped him again. He wanted to struggle, but his hands were tied behind his back. He tried to open his eyes, but a strip of cloth blocked his vision. By looking downward toward a bright triangle, he could just make out the wet ground at the base of the post and the sight of his own muddy boots, whose laces had been removed the evening before so he couldn't hang himself in his cell. His heart started racing in his chest. In the silence, a man to his right burst into sobs. Another started screaming insults, cursing his comrades.

Charles heard the metallic clack of the rifle bolts slamming the bullets into the chambers.

He straightened and turned his head to the right, toward where the generals and the chaplain would be standing. Then he spat in their direction with all his might.

21

"I'LL NEVER GET THROUGH this book!" Eric groaned. "It's huge!"

"It's the best volume available on the Spanish Civil War," said the bookstore clerk.

Gilles smiled and shrugged.

"See? You don't have any choice."

He picked up the book and turned it over to check the price.

"It's 149 francs. I'll buy it for you."

"You can pay for it at the register," said the clerk, turning to a carton full of new arrivals. "Have a nice day."

They took a few steps between the bookshelves, then Eric grabbed his brother's sleeve and said, "You're out of your mind, paying 149 francs for a book I won't even read!"

"We'll see," said Gilles philosophically. "Let's just say it's an investment in your future."

"Man, your time in Bosnia has screwed you up, but good. I still don't get what you're after."

Gilles paid and let his brother carry the bag. They went out into the street.

"Want to come with me? I have to report in by two o'clock."

"Sure. But I can guarantee I'm not going to read this book of yours. All I wanted was for you to explain what happened at Guernica."

"What do you want to know about it, exactly? And why are you so interested all of a sudden?"

"Oh, no real reason... I guess I heard it mentioned on TV."

"I don't know where to start. I can't just give you a quickie seminar about it. Guernica was a little town like any other until April 1937, when the German air force turned it to ashes. It was such a massacre that since then, the name Guernica has been associated in people's memory with everything that's horrible about war. Particularly because Picasso painted *Guernica* that year. It's his most famous painting, and rightly so."

Eric pulled the book out of the bag and looked at it. The Picasso painting was reproduced on the cover. Amid the jumble of strong lines, he could make out a distorted woman, her arms raised to the sky, and the mouth of a terrified horse, dripping foam. It hadn't looked like that at all, he thought to himself.

"What the heck were the Germans doing in Spain in 1937, anyway? I thought the Second World War didn't start until 1939."

"It was a rehearsal for their grand strategy. They

were testing their equipment and the passivity of the other European countries."

"But why Spain?"

"Because the country was in the middle of a civil war between the Republicans and the Nationalists. Franco, the right-wing Nationalist general, asked Hitler for material help, and that included the famous Condor Legion that bombed Guernica."

"Condor?"

As they walked along, Gilles took the book from his brother's hands, checked the list of illustrations, then held the volume out to him. The Condor Legion insignia could be seen on a banner: in the middle of an iron cross, a condor with outspread wings clutched a swastika in its talons.

A long moment of silence followed, which Gilles finally broke. "Something the matter?"

His gaze vacant, Eric looked away from the page. He didn't answer.

"You've already seen this insignia somewhere before, haven't you?" asked Gilles.

Eric nodded.

"Where?"

On a computer screen, Eric thought to himself. On a fighter plane's fuselage. Aloud, he said: "On a pal's jacket, last week."

A week... Eric suddenly realized that barely a week had gone by since they had visited the games store, and that during that week everything he believed in had been overturned. Somehow, they had to go back to before all this happened, to a time when everything was still simple, with no dangers or hidden meanings. How did the old man know? he wondered. Why did he give us the game? To corrupt us? To test us? As these questions raced through his mind, he was horrified to realize that at this point the only way to answer them might be to go on playing the game.

"On whose jacket?" Gilles repeated.

"Andreas's."

Gilles' face clouded. "I'm not surprised," he muttered through clenched teeth. "I should have guessed."

"Hey, don't get carried away. It's just a decoration, something for show."

The excuse sounded lame and unconvincing, even to Eric's ears. A week ago, the attitude of the old man in the store had astonished him. Now, he wasn't sure of anything anymore. If that insignia was associated in people's memories with massacres as bloody as the one he had lived through, how could anyone imagine wearing it on a jacket lapel "for show"? Didn't the very fact that he would openly display such a symbol of death and destruction suggest something darker and more cowardly?

"It's not 'just a decoration,'" Gilles said firmly, as if echoing the thoughts in his brother's mind. "It's a Nazi insignia, and even if Andreas doesn't know all its history, he's well aware of what that medal implies, both for people on his side and for their victims, believe me."

"He says it's just part of a collection, like my collection of pogs, or your collection of badges three years ago."

"My badge collection... Hmm, I forgot about that. But those are completely different. They're just fads, expensive trinkets. For a few weeks you think you can't live without them, and then they're forgotten. No, Andreas knows perfectly well what he's doing, especially since you can't find that sort of garbage just anywhere."

"I don't follow you," broke in Eric, who didn't know why he kept arguing with his brother.

Each one of Gilles's remarks seemed right and found an echo of truth in himself, but they made the path Andreas was on all the more troubling. Against all evidence, Eric would have liked to convince himself that his friend just had an unusual sense of humor and a taste for the outrageous.

"I don't follow you," he repeated. "Andreas has the right to like uniforms and fantasize about the army. Even you…"

"Stop right there," warned Gilles. "You're about to say something really stupid. I didn't go to Bosnia because I liked the army or because the idea of slogging through mud in fatigues gave me a hard-on. Or because I dreamed of cradling a machine gun in my arms. I went there because I wasn't able to avoid being drafted, and imagined — and I do mean imagined — that I might be useful to something or somebody over there.

"What your pal Andreas wants is what the people on the other end of that bridge I was guarding had: the grandiose sense of power that holding a weapon gives to every sorry son of a bitch who doesn't have a clue, doesn't have any guts, who doesn't have anything except his hatred for himself and other people. Andreas can blather on about how noble the military is and the glory of serving the flag, but it's a bunch of bullshit he doesn't even understand. His family has been spoon-feeding him that crap ever since he was a baby, using words to hide the main thing: the desire to destroy, crush, and kill.

"During the Spanish Civil War, the fascist side came up with a rallying cry that captured this perfectly: *Viva la muerte!* Long live death! Down with intellectuals, down with thought, long live nothing-ness... That's what they're after, Andreas and all the rest of those assholes who parade around pretending to represent the spirit of past wars while they're really just looking forward to the next killing fields."

"What makes you say his family taught him that?"

"You should read the newspapers sometime, you ignoramus. Andreas's father is a real piece of shit, ripe and smelly."

"Mr. Salaun? But he works at city hall, and he ran for some office or other..."

"For the Assembly, a few years ago. And he'll run in the next elections, never fear. He'll be there. His suit will be a little tighter, his hair a little greasier, but he'll be there. And one of these days, if everyone keeps spacing out in front of their video games, he'll finally get elected. 'All that is necessary for the forces of evil to win in this world is for enough good men to do nothing.'"

"Did you make that up?"

"Nope, it wasn't me, but no matter — it says it all. Well, here's where I turn off."

Puzzled, Eric looked around. The army barracks were another two miles further, on the outskirts of town.

"We may not see each other again for a while,"

said Gilles. "I don't think I'll be able to get another leave for a long time."

"But where are you going? This isn't the…"

"I'm going there," said Gilles, pointing to a large red-brick building separated from the street by a high fence and a wide, shady lawn.

"There? But that's where…"

"Where the nut cases live? Go on! The psychos, the wackos, the raving loonies…"

"Stop it!" shouted Eric.

He was paralyzed with fear and confusion. Gilles stopped teasing him, and continued in a calmer tone.

"It's the county psychiatric hospital. The army sends soldiers suffering from psychic traumas to the doctors who study stress syndrome."

"But… when will you get out?"

"I don't know. When I'm sure things are better on the outside. It may take a while."

Gilles put his arms around his brother in a brief, fierce hug, then released him.

"Hey, don't worry about me. Put your energy into your Spanish Civil War. And come see me if you have questions."

"Can you have visitors?"

"Of course; this isn't the Middle Ages. It's a public hospital."

Gilles backed away, turned on his heel, and walked through the hospital gate. Still reeling from the shock, Eric watched as he hurried along the main path, occasionally stepping around a wheelchair or a patient in a bathrobe soliloquizing to a flower-bed. Before disappearing under a stone arch, Gilles turned around one last time and raised his arm to the sky, fist clenched.

Eric hesitated, raised his arm for an ordinary wave, then imitated his brother.

"No pasarán!" yelled Gilles, using the slogan of the Spanish resistance: They will not pass!

Long after Gilles had disappeared, his laughter echoed from beneath the arch.

22

"WELL, WELL, WELL, if it isn't our good buddy the commander! Now that you're here, our touching family reunion is complete."

Andreas had spoken without getting up from the brown leatherette armchair he was sprawled in, his muddy Doc Martens propped on Charles's bed-spread. Eric closed the hospital room door behind him. Charles, who was standing by the bed, was un-hurriedly packing his few toilet articles in a gym bag. When he saw Eric, a broad smile lit up his face.

Though surprised and embarrassed by Andreas's sarcastic presence, Eric didn't let it get to him. But there was something odd about Charles's smile. His face was still the same, a bit too pale and impassive, with the same Coke-bottle glasses that made him look confused. But his smile had changed, become firmer. In the two days Charles had spent in the hospital, he seemed to have turned into somebody else. Or maybe he was the same Charles, but more mature and less fearful. Without being fully con-scious of all this, Eric felt at a loss, as if their trio's secret hierarchy had suddenly changed and he had been cast in the role of killjoy.

"So, you recovered from the pasting I gave you?

Son of a bitch, you should have seen it, dude. I gave those pathetic Commies a grade-A whipping. The mother of all ass-kickings! He didn't have a building left standing, not a truck, not a road. I *pulverized* him!"

"We didn't have any anti-aircraft defense! You didn't even warn me it wasn't a ground attack… I didn't have the slightest chance. That isn't a game, it's murder!"

"Aww, the boy's gonna start bawling. He's so sensitive!"

"And you didn't have to use incendiary bombs, either. We had no way of fighting back."

"Ah, the incendiaries. I love the noise the bomb bays make when they open, a sort of hydraulic whisper… *Whoooshhh…* And the rumble the bombs make when they hit their target. It's a little like in the commercial: the first wave of Heinkel 52 fighters passes over, then the second wave of Heinkel 111 bombers fries the Commies before they know what hit 'em."

"Hey, glad you enjoyed it so much," said Eric. "You want to go on? Don't let me stand in your way. But you better ask yourself if you aren't going a little too far. When do you plan to stop? You know, when the novelty of aerial massacres starts to wear off, what do you try next? Torture? Rape?"

"Oh, stop it," moaned Andreas. "I'm creaming my jeans."

"Anyway, I'm done with all that. What about you, Charles?"

"Me, too. We went too far."

Andreas sighed and forced a smile. "Hey, wait a minute, guys, I don't get it. You're really gonna be such sore losers?"

"It isn't just a game for me," said Charles. "Not anymore."

Something in his voice suggested suffering and a new strength. Relieved, Eric joined in: "It isn't a game for me anymore, either. And if you could just be honest with us for two seconds, you'd admit it hasn't been a game for you for a long time now."

"What are you saying, you mental degenerate?"

"Your insignia, in the old guy's shop in London..."

"What about it?"

"It's the insignia of the Condor Legion. It's a Nazi insignia."

"So what, ass-wipe? That stuff's all historical. It's a collector's item, get it? I know guys who would kill to have one."

"Well, that doesn't say much for the people you hang out with. Anyway, from now on you can play S.S. all by yourself."

"Don't get mad, you jerk. It tears me up to admit it, but I love playing against you. I love watching those little Soviet bitches running through the flames, with their hair catching fire, and then their tit-slings…"

"Go fuck yourself," spat Eric.

"Hey, don't get all huffy," hissed Andreas. "Just imagine what could happen if you piss off the Frag-meister, if you take away his shiny new toy. What if I decide to find out what it's like for real…? Suppose I want to see what your Bosanski princess looks like with a few pounds of burning sodium chlorate in her cute little dime-store book bag? I wonder what a barbecued Muslim chick tastes like… Guess there's no telling, right? Probably like sausage, even if she doesn't eat pork."

Andreas yelped as Eric's fist smacked the grin off his face. He raised his arms to protect himself and shoved the other boy back. Charles stepped between them.

"That's enough, you guys. You're nuts."

"This is between me and him, Joan of Arc. Get your ass out of the way!"

Charles shook his head. Just then, the bedroom door opened and Mrs. Boisdeffre came in. "Everything's ready, darling; the paperwork is all taken care of. Oh, you two are here, too? It's sweet of you to visit Charles, but you mustn't tire him out."

"Mother, please…"

"I know, I know, you aren't a baby anymore. But you gave us quite a scare."

"Excuse me, gotta get going," muttered Andreas as he made his way to the door. "But it's no big deal. We'll meet again soon, I promise. *Auf wiedersehen!*"

"Networked together?" murmured Charles. "How the heck could you have played in network mode against him? Our computers aren't connected."

As a precaution, Eric closed his friend's bedroom door, to shut them away from Mr. and Mrs. Boisdeffre. During the drive home, and in spite of Charles's amused protests, his mother's face tightened with fear whenever they started talking, even in a round-about way, about the last game session between Andreas and Eric.

"I know that," said Eric. "That's what I've been racking my brains trying to understand. We didn't play side-by-side, or taking turns. Andreas was at his place and I was here. I was typing on the keyboard when he contacted me."

Charles looked behind his computer, then shook his head.

"It's… it's impossible, and you know it as well as I do."

"Well, what happened to you is impossible, too."

"Yeah, but there are lots of ways to explain it. If I told a grown-up like Doctor Munier about it, he'd say I just invented that spring of 1917, that I must have read about it somewhere and my feelings of guilt created some sort of waking nightmare."

"And you call that a reasonable explanation?"

"I'm not looking for reasonable, I'm trying to understand how the game works, and where it's going to take us…"

"What do you mean, 'where it's going to take us'? I thought you never wanted to play it again."

Charles came over and sat down next to Eric. He pulled the thick book about the Spanish Civil War out of the bag.

"Do you really think," Charles asked grimly, "that Andreas won't carry out his threats?"

23

SLEEP HAD DESERTED Eric in the hours before dawn. He tossed and turned in his bed, dozing fitfully as the minutes ticked by. Finally, at around nine o'clock, unable to stand it, he got up and took a cold shower to clear his head. "How can I tell her?" he wondered for the umpteenth time. "How can I get Elena to understand that she could be in danger, without sounding like a nut case?" He was just finishing shaving with his brother's razor when the doorbell rang. The television's volume dropped and his mother's voice called from the end of the hallway: "That must be the physiotherapist. Have him wait in the living room. I'm not ready."

Rolling his eyes, Eric quickly wiped off the streaks of bloody shaving cream decorating his chin. He headed for the apartment's front door, buttoning his shirt as he went. The night before, Dr. Munier had spent a quarter of an hour at his mother's bedside, taking advantage of one of her regular distress calls to deliver some straight talk. He made her promise to undergo a dozen physiotherapy sessions to get her walking again, and thereby regain some autonomy.

As the doctor was leaving, he had glanced into

Eric's bedroom and found him sitting at his table with the computer turned off and a book open in front of him. Munier lifted the cover and gave a brief nod of approval.

"*Man's Hope* by Malraux. Is that on your reading list?"

"No, not exactly. It's my brother's."

"Gilles? How is he?"

"He… he was home on leave. I walked him back to the base yesterday."

Doctor Munier seemed about to say something, but changed his mind.

"Are you interested in the Spanish Civil War, too?"

"Too?"

"Yes, like Gilles. Hasn't he talked about it to you? That's one reason he volunteered to go to Bosnia."

Seeing Eric's puzzled look, the doctor set down his bag and took a seat.

"Do you mind?" he asked, helping himself to a stick of chewing gum from a pack on the table. "I'm surprised he hasn't mentioned it. Gilles is fascinated by the International Brigades; he's borrowed several of my books about them. You know he wants to be a history teacher, like my wife?"

"Yeah, sure, but I never knew… Well, I didn't

make the connection before. In fact, I still don't get it."

"Is this the first book you've read about the Spanish Civil War? You don't know anything else about it?"

"Guernica. I know Guernica."

"Sure," said Munier. "Everybody knows about Guernica."

Eric didn't dare contradict him.

"Gilles thinks the situation in Bosnia today is very close to the situation in Spain in 1936, and he's probably right. Of course, the same powers aren't involved and the stakes are different, but according to him, people's attitudes today are exactly the same as those of our grandparents. For the last fifty years we've said over and over that if we had only known what was going to happen, Hitler would never have been able to get so far. Yet today, with all the world's crimes being shown live on television, we're *still* just as passive. Maybe more so, because seeing that garbage day after day makes us numb.

"You know, I'm barely forty years old, but I grew up in a time you can't even imagine, where there wasn't any television, or not much. A time when thoughts had time to ripen, when people read more books than they do today. I didn't know anything about all this," said Munier, gesturing toward the computer. "Video games, all this virtual stuff... I don't have anything against it, but it's a world that's beyond *this* world, beyond what's *real*, a place to *escape* from reality.

"When I was your age and headed for medical school, we were all very political. We were hip to everything that was going on in the world, and we still thought we could change the society we lived in. Your brother's a bit like that, even if it's out of fashion... Maybe you've seen that disgusting commercial for some video game system or other... You see people from my generation, with hair down to their shoulders, leading a demonstration and throwing rocks at the cops. And the tag line says, 'Well, you had to do something to pass the time, before SEGA.'"

Munier shrugged.

"I'm sorry, I'm boring you with my war stories. And I'm in no position to preach. It isn't a matter of generations. Your brother has probably done more to live according to his beliefs than I ever will."

The doctor had made Eric promise to get his mother to make an appointment with the physiotherapist that very afternoon, then left.

Eric hurried down the hallway and opened the door to find Elena standing on the landing. They looked at each other for a moment while Eric's mother again repeated, from deep inside the apartment: "Ask him to wait in the living room."

"It isn't the therapist..." Eric finally called back. "It's... it's a friend. I'm going outside to talk!" he added, closing the door behind him.

"I came to talk to you," said Elena, a statement so painfully obvious that they both smiled.

"It'd be better if we went for a walk," said Eric. "The place is a mess, especially my room."

Elena nodded and turned, followed by Eric.

"You're bleeding," she said in a soft voice as they were heading downstairs.

"It's nothing," he answered, searching his pockets for something to wipe his chin with. What must I look like? he wondered desperately. I look like a jerk who doesn't even know how to use a razor. In fact, I *am* a jerk who doesn't know how to use a razor!

The street was empty, and they walked aimlessly. Eric would have liked it to start raining, so he could again use bad weather as an excuse to press close to her. Just as the thought crossed his mind, Elena turned and gave him a smile that petrified him. He had the panicky feeling that she knew exactly what he was thinking.

"You must have thought I was crazy the other night," she said.

He was ready to agree with anything she said, but in this case, he didn't even know what she was talking about. Why the hell was he always so slow on the uptake when he was with her?

"Oh, no. Not really."

"I ran off without a word of explanation, without even saying goodbye. I didn't want you to think it was your fault."

"Oh, no…" said Eric.

He would have given his right arm for a clever remark, but nothing came to mind.

"I had… I had a weird experience with your friend's computer."

Eric felt a shiver run up his spine, just like in novels.

"What kind of experience?"

"I saw something… that is, I think I saw something… It was like a newsreel about my country, only it wasn't a movie. It was… different."

"Was it violent?" Eric asked.

"Horrible," she answered. "As long as I live, I'll never forget what I saw."

Her voice was trembling, and Eric wanted to take her in his arms — and before he realized what was happening, he had. A jangle of alarm bells and sirens went off in his head. Then Elena's lips met his, and he didn't hear anything more. I did it! he thought. By the god of super-bonus points and free extra games, I did it!

When Eric finally let her go, he realized they were kissing in the middle of a street in his town that he felt he had never seen before. A wave of emotion flooded over him, until the moment when Elena said, "You're so cute."

The tone of her words crucified him. She sounded affectionately teasing, as if she were talking to a kitten instead of a magnificent lover. Instinctively, Eric knew he had lost her, that his dream had just shattered.

He smiled, because smiling was the thing to do. And he slipped into the role of faithful protector, in order to remove any importance from the kiss. At that moment Eric realized he had a soul, because it was screaming. He relaxed his grip on Elena, went on walking at her side, forced himself to be casual — while an inconsolable part of himself tried to understand how and at what moment she had removed herself from him.

"Your friend's computer," Elena continued. "Does it run all by itself?"

"Not really. It's hooked up with other computers. Why?"

"I don't know how it could have happened, but as I was looking at the screen, the computer started

143

up, and I saw something that only I could have seen. As if it were meant just for me."

Eric felt a sudden jolt in his chest.

"That's... that's what I wanted to talk to you about. Someone took control of Charles's computer, and mine too, at the same time. A boy in our class. I know this is gonna sound weird, but you have to watch out for him."

"Who is it?"

"Andreas."

"Andreas? But why? I thought you guys were friends."

"I thought so, too, but I was wrong."

"But what does this have to do with me? And how could he send me those images?"

"It's hard to explain. It isn't really Andreas who sent them. I think the computer sends us images that are inside us, only they're hidden. It makes us face things we don't want to see."

"But I've never done anything to Andreas. I've never even spoken to him."

"He just doesn't like people like you," mumbled Eric.

"People like me?"

"Muslims," said Eric with embarrassment. As he said it, he realized he had no idea what the word actually meant.

Elena stopped. Eric turned to her, ready to face her anger, but he saw only puzzlement in her eyes. Then she gave a bitter laugh. "But I'm not Muslim, I'm a Serb. And my father's a Serb."

"I don't think he makes that distinction. To him, you're a foreigner."

"And to you?"

To himself, Eric thought, You're foreign to me, too, because I fell in love with you without understanding anything about you. Aloud, he said, "No, I don't think the way he does. But I didn't know. I thought... Anyway, my brother went to Bosnia with the army... I thought it was the Muslims who became refugees because of the war, so I figured..."

"Because you think there are people who like war, who like to wallow in it? Everybody wants to flee war, except the people who enjoy making it. And you can find them in every country, under every flag, in every family. My father's that way. Your brother..."

"My brother isn't anything like that!" Eric cut in with sudden vehemence. "My brother went there to be useful, to help people."

Elena's skepticism could be seen in her eyes.

"My brother hates war," Eric insisted. "Just talk to him, and you'll see."

"What's the point?" she said, shrugging her shoulders.

"Because you don't have the right to judge him before you've even met him."

She searched a long time for an answer, but in the end she silently agreed. They didn't exchange another word before reaching Elena's building. Giving him a peck on the cheek, she turned to go.

"Muslim?" she called out as she climbed the stairs, and burst out laughing, a laugh that brought tears to her eyes. "Wait 'til I tell my dad *that* one…"

"Did she use her tongue?" murmured a honeyed voice at the other end of the line.

An irrational fear swept over Eric.

"Did she stick her tongue in you? Shit, man, you've gone mute. She must have swallowed your tonsils."

"Andreas?"

"He speaks! It's a miracle, doctor, he's saved!"

"Why don't you just leave us alone?"

"Is that any way to talk to an old friend? And you haven't answered my question, dude. How was it? She didn't taste too spicy for you?"

"What are you raving about, you sleazebag?"

"Oh, so now it's insults, huh? You really disappoint me. I wouldn't have expected that from you."

"Can't you leave us alone? We don't want to play your shitty little game anymore."

"That's assuming you have a choice, dickhead. You'd do better to get yourself ready. I'll be waiting for you at seven o'clock tonight at Boadilla del Monte, on the outskirts of Madrid."

"Not a chance."

"My, my, you must have a virus! You aren't formatted right! Do I have to dot the i's and cross the t's for you? I followed the two of you in the street. I saw you mop the boogers out of her nose with your tongue. So now I know where she lives, jerk-off!"

There was silence on the line for a moment, then Andreas hammered his message home again.

"Seven o'clock sharp at Boadilla del Monte. Or else your little princess could be the lead story on the evening news."

24

"IF WE GIVE IN to his blackmail," repeated Eric, "nothing will stop him from doing it again until hell freezes over."

"That's not certain," said Charles, checking the spines of the books he had borrowed from the town library that morning.

"But even if we win the battle, it won't put Andreas out of action. He'll just want to fight us again tomorrow."

"Maybe. But we know some things he doesn't, things he hasn't taken the time to learn."

"You think those *books* are going to save us?"

"I'm not talking about books. The books only give us a slight advantage, by giving us a better idea of the opposing forces. I'm talking about the game itself, about the experience we've gotten from it. I used to think you could win in a strategy game just by analyzing the objective data: terrain, weather conditions, weapons of the opposing forces. But if we just stick to those, we'll lose for sure. The Nationalists are better armed, they have the benefit of Nazi material support, they're better trained…"

"Thanks for cheering me up."

"But until I got drawn into the game myself, I

had always overlooked something essential. I saw my units as pawns that I could array on a map, and pull back or send to their deaths, as I pleased. For that matter, that's how the generals on both sides played out World War I."

"Played?"

"Yes, played. What difference was there between them and us? Sitting back at headquarters, they would decide to mobilize such-and-such an infantry unit and send it to attack the front at such-and-such a place. Then they paused the game so they could go have dinner and get a good night's sleep."

"What are you saying?"

"I'm trying to get a point across. About what I learned before I was shot by the firing squad, and what you learned when the bombs were falling around you. It's one of the two secret weapons we have to defeat Andreas."

"So tell me!"

"Each of our units, each of those little black dots on the screen, is a human being."

Bent over the computer, Eric scrunched up his eyes.

"Wait a minute. *That's* your revelation?"

Charles nodded, lost in contemplation of the screen, on which miniature armored columns were moving to surround Madrid.

"I can't believe this!" Eric exploded. "You think some bullshit philosophical maxim is going to help us beat Andreas? 'Each of our units represents a human being'? Sounds to me like you really did have an epileptic fit!"

"You aren't listening to what I'm saying. You're reacting the way Andreas does, the way I used to. To him, those units are just pawns, to be manipulated any way he likes. The game lets him incarnate specific people so he can enjoy the destruction he's causing from close up. Sort of like having a front-row seat. That's what turns him on. But you and I know that even in this virtual universe, each character has his own life, his own reasons for fighting or surrendering. An individual value that can't be reduced to a number of life points, or physical strength, or weaponry. And *that*, Andreas doesn't understand."

"Boy, that's brilliant. That really gives us some edge over Andreas's tanks and bombers, all right. It might even be unfair…"

He tapped on the keyboard, and a picture of their troops appeared onscreen: nine men, lined up as if for a class photograph. Except for one of them, they looked barely older than the two boys. Eric's heart sank. He examined their faces, suddenly silenced by the terrible realization that what Charles had just said was true.

The men all looked exhausted. Despite their youth, bluish-grey stubble covered the lower part of their faces. The first snowflakes were depositing a thin, shroud-like layer of ice on their greasy hair and the collars of their jackets. Their weapons, if you could use the word to dignify the jumble of unlikely pop-guns and rusty grenades, appeared at the bottom of the screen, ready to be distributed.

"It might even be unfair to fight Andreas with such an advantage," Eric repeated. "After all, according to your books, all he has is two battalions of veteran troops plus the German and Italian armory."

"Yes, but deep down, you know that isn't what's going to count this time. Franco has decided to recapture Boadilla because it's on the last road the Republicans can use to resupply Madrid during the siege. If Boadilla falls, Madrid falls…"

"So what difference do you think it'll make? Franco will win his war, and the Nazis will win with him."

"The only battles that are lost at the outset are the ones you refuse to fight."

"Oh, great! First it's philosophy, now it's Buddhist quotations."

"We can keep Andreas from taking Boadilla," insisted Charles. "Or at least we can keep him from taking it today."

"Well, so what? He'll take it tomorrow, or the day after! I read all about it; it's a done deal. Madrid's gonna fall!"

"You're forgetting the most important thing. Look at these men. Really look at them!" said Charles, grabbing Eric by the arm. "For them, nothing is settled yet. It's a December morning a few days before Christmas. They belong to the 12th International Brigade, or what's left of it. They've been holding this village for weeks and they have no intention of giving it up. They aren't concerned with history. Anyway, they don't know it because it hasn't been written yet. And even if they knew all was already lost... Look at them. Do they look like guys who are going to give up without a fight?"

Eric didn't answer. He gazed at the men's faces, trying to guess which one of them he would incarnate during the game.

"And we have another advantage, a second element that Andreas doesn't know about," murmured Charles, as if afraid of being overheard.

Eric turned toward him, searching his face. Charles kept his eyes lowered.

"This afternoon, after you called to warn me about Andreas's ultimatum, I tried to enter the game. I wanted to reconnoiter the terrain and to see if I could scare up some extra ammunition."

"So what happened?"

"I couldn't get in."

"What do you mean?"

"I can't access the game anymore. I can mobilize a few units from the outside, like in a normal strategy game, but only in a very superficial way. I can't incarnate any of the fighters anymore."

"You mean to say I'm gonna have to face him alone? You call that an advantage?"

"Just think for a moment. In your last session, Andreas completely defeated you in the Guernica bombing, but your character survived, right?"

"Yeah…"

"But me, I died in the game, in 1917. And I can't access it anymore."

Eric nodded, looking thoughtful.

Charles went on slowly, as if he were trying to convince himself. "This means that even if you don't hold Boadilla, you only have to kill Andreas's character to keep him from playing anymore. You don't have to win the Spanish Civil War, Eric. You don't even have to hold the village."

"All I have to do…"

Charles finished the thought: "…is eliminate Andreas."

25

IT HAD SNOWED all night long. Stiff with cold and damp, Esmond Romilly was relieved of guard duty around three in the morning by Joe. An Irishman slightly older than Esmond, Joe's claim to fame within the company was his ability to belch to the tune of "God Save the Queen." Esmond handed him his rifle, a Springfield he had gotten from a Fascist deserter and whose good working condition was in marked contrast to most of their weapons. To see him through the night, Joe gave him his pistol, a rusty 1896 German Mauser whose trigger tended to jam in cold weather. Esmond put the gun in his pocket and slowly walked down the hill to the village in the pale moonlight, taking care not to slip on a patch of ice or frozen shit. Even in its glory days, Boadilla del Monte had never had a sewer or drainage system, and it now seemed doubtful it ever would. He reached the bottom of the hill without any trouble and walked through the sleeping village's narrow streets. Skirting the bullet-pocked church wall, Esmond ducked through a gaping shell-hole and entered the sacristy. He stepped over a statue, its features smashed into anonymity by rifle butts, and circled the fire pit, where the last planks of the confessional booth were burning. He lay down on his pallet fully clothed. With fingers stiff with cold despite his double gloves, he clumsily gripped the blanket and pulled it up to his chin, heedless of its hordes of resident lice. He fell into an exhausted sleep and dreamed of a strange world in which he was sitting at a table in front of a dark screen in a room awash with light.

The Fascists attacked at dawn. The first shell whistled over the trenches and smashed into a vacant house near the Comitad de Guerra. Esmond opened his eyes, saw the ceiling of the nave at a dizzying height above him, and thought for a moment that he was in free-fall toward the sky. As he lay tensely on his pallet, the silence in the church was broken by shouts from everywhere:

"Fascistas! Fascistas!"

A second shell fell nearby and the shock shattered one of the last unbroken stained-glass windows above the altar. Esmond leaped out of his bedding, ran to the door, and raced up the hill to the trenches. Today's the day, he thought. Today's the day they decided to attack.

For the past three days, columns of armored vehicles had been preparing to besiege the village, deploying men and equipment along a front less than eight hundred yards from the Republican trenches. When Esmond reached the top of the hill, he was astonished at the metamorphosis brought by the night's snowfall. The devastated fields, which had been drowning in mud and feces, were now covered with an immaculate layer of white. The forest that protected part of the road below looked like something on a postcard.

It briefly occurred to him that it was December 20, and that in just five days his parents would gather around the Christmas tree in their large house in London's East End. In front of a mantelpiece crowded with Christmas cards from another era, they would pray for their son's safety. If I die today, Esmond thought, they won't hear about it for weeks, if at all. It had been a long time since he last thought about death. His main worries these last three months had been, in descending order of importance: firewood, food, vermin, oil to clean his rifle with, and last — way down at the bottom of the list — the enemy.

His battalion's second company had reached Boadilla early in November without encountering any resistance. Helped by the village militia, it had held the main road and suffered no casualties aside from two men who were injured when defective cartridges exploded in their own rifles. Esmond hadn't fired a single shot since his arrival in Boadilla, and he had only one fear, that of being hurt in an accident before facing the enemy. Unlike many of the militiamen, for whom having any kind of weapon was cause for celebration, Esmond had taken great care to acquire decent equipment over the last two months. During a fog-shrouded sortie into no man's land, he had practically tripped over a deserter, a peasant in his fifties who had been drafted into the Nationalist ranks against his will. The man gave Esmond his rifle. Followed by his "prisoner," he had then crept as far as the road a few dozen yards from the enemy lines, to retrieve something he had coveted ever since he spotted it a few days before but which he had never been able to reach: a cartridge belt abandoned in a trench during an enemy battalion's hurried withdrawal. He had taken risks that in any other circumstance he would have judged foolhardy, because experience had taught him that he couldn't rely on the bullets they'd been issued when they enlisted in the Republican ranks. Enemy cartridges, especially German ones, were considered real war treasures.

Slipping his left hand into his pocket, Esmond fingered the metal cartridge clip he always kept in reserve, then realized with dismay that he'd given his rifle to Joe.

Reaching the trenches, Esmond lunged forward

to dodge enemy machine-gun fire. Despite the blanket of snow, the bitter smell of piss and shit filled his throat, and, as always, nearly made him vomit. I'll never get used to it, he thought, and the incongruous notion struck him that it was possible, both literally and figuratively, that he would never have a chance to. He stood up: the trench was empty. Behind him, he heard a clamor from the village. He glanced back to see a human tide — women armed with pitchforks or black flags and peasants brandishing carbines — climbing the hill. Two mortar rounds landed in the center of the ragtag crowd, splashing the snow with pieces of bodies, earth, and blood.

Turning to face the enemy lines, Esmond saw the other eight members of his company who had taken cover among the trees below him. He leaped from the trench and ran to join them. Bullets whistled around him, which he avoided by losing his balance and tumbling down the slope on his back, gripping Joe's Mauser.

As Esmond gathered his wits, he saw Jurgen Messer, the anti-Nazi German who had come to fight alongside the Republicans, step from behind a tree and lob a black metal disk high into the air. The grenade described a majestic arc, and — as Jurgen took the first bullet full in the chest and did a shaky two-step in the snow, trying to get his balance — it dropped right onto the fascist mortar emplacement. For a long instant nothing happened, and Esmond's heart tightened. He watched as Jurgen fell, thinking that his friend had died for nothing. Then, inexplicably, the grenade decided to explode. With a dull thud, it demolished the mortar and its servers. Esmond's entire company rushed forward under cover of the smoke cloud to attack the two machine guns. They got as far as the road before being pinned down by enemy fire. The noise was deafening. A storm of lead seemed to be breaking over them. From time to time, in the middle of the thunder of explosions, he heard a curse from an overexcited militiaman behind them:

"Fascistas! Maricones!"

To keep his terror at bay, Esmond took up the cry, screaming it as he ran toward the shell-hole where Joe was hunkered down.

"The machine gun," said Joe.

They exchanged a feverish glance, then charged. Time seemed to stop. Nothing but shouts and sudden explosions. The sky tilted above their heads. When his vision cleared, Esmond was kneeling near the wreckage of the first German machine gun, his bayonet sunk up to the hilt into the body of a Falangist. He shoved the enemy corpse back and had time to notice that the man, who was about thirty, was wearing a brand-new uniform, with an impeccable fatigue jacket and a black cap to which was pinned a grinning skull over a swastika. Esmond raised his head to speak to Joe. His friend was kneeling halfway up the slope, the Springfield in his hands pointed to the ground. His head was bent down to his chest at a horrible angle. For just a moment, that was all Esmond thought about. Not about the bullets, or the place where they were, or even the fact that Joe was dead. He was thinking that it wasn't normal, or even conceivable, that Joe's head should stay in that position. He crawled over to his friend and put his hand on Joe's cheek, as if to help him raise his head. Just then a burst of gunfire hit Joe in the chest, pinning them both to the ground. Recovering his wits, Esmond grabbed the rifle and tore it from Joe's dead fingers.

"Get back," yelled Tich Adderley. "Everybody! Quick! Hurry up! Get back!"

Esmond stood up and retreated. He didn't stop when he reached the edge of the wood. He didn't stop when Tich, gesturing frantically to his comrades, took a bullet in the head and collapsed. He didn't even stop when he burst into Boadilla's main street, stumbling over its dozens of corpses. The

Germans had regrouped, set up their other two mortar batteries, and adjusted their aim. The village was collapsing around him. As Esmond staggered, dazed, across the town square, he was struck by a strange memory, the memory of another village, like this one, being leveled by a bombardment. This was followed by an absurd thought: *I have to kill him. I have to find out who he is, and kill him.*

The Fascists had taken the village, or what was left of it. In the distance, shots and explosions could be heard, but Esmond doubted that reinforcements could come from Brunete or Madrid in time to save the last holdouts. He lay down on the church tower floor, crawled under the bronze bell to the metal railing, and raised his head. Some fifteen Legionnaires and Falangists had taken the main square and were searching through the rubble. One of them kicked an old woman in black who was curled up on the ground. When she moaned, the man leaned over, put the muzzle of his Luger on her neck, and fired. Esmond took a moment to relax his tense muscles, then braced his rifle on the tower railing. The man appeared in his sights. Esmond saw him turn around to joke with one of his companions. The bullet cut short his sniggering. In the square, three more men fell before the Fascists were able to take cover. Esmond threw himself backward, hoping against hope that they hadn't seen him. In any case, he thought, short of firing a cannon at the tower, they didn't have much chance of dislodging him from his perch.

That was when he heard a long whistling inside the church, as if an asthmatic dragon was catching its breath. There was silence, then the sound of footsteps on the tower stairs. They had located him. He carefully went down a few steps, heard the same breathing noise, a scream, and then a hurried clatter in the staircase. Some of the survivors must have taken refuge in the church with him, and were now being pursued by the Fascists inside the tower. The thought occurred to Esmond that maybe he hadn't been spotted, that all he might have to do was to stay motionless... Then a child screamed, right below him, a scream of pure terror. The breathing came again, more powerful now, more menacing. Esmond forced himself to descend a few steps to meet the dragon. A voice rang out: a voice that, strangely enough, he seemed to recognize.

"Here, chick-chick-chick. Come to papa..."

Esmond's heart was pounding like a trip-hammer in his chest. He stepped onto the tower's first-floor landing, only to find a girl about ten years old huddled in a dark corner behind a pile of crushed organ pipes.

"Here, chicky-chicky," repeated the voice, and the dragon shot a tongue of flame up the staircase.

The fireball rolled through the air a few yards from Esmond, burning his eyebrows and scorching the fuzz on his wool jacket. A smell of burning flesh filled his nostrils as a crazed, joyless laugh barked in the stairwell. *And before he even saw him, Esmond knew he was the one.*

The little girl, who was cowering in the shadows, looked pleadingly at him. Esmond would have liked to have the strength to smile at her, give her some little sign of solidarity, but he was too frightened. Eyes wide, he aimed the Springfield at the stairs and took a stand with his back to the stone wall. If the dragon belched another tongue of flame, he would burn to death without being able to fire a single shot, but it was the only chance he had of wounding it, maybe killing it.

In his hand, the rifle's grip was sticky with sweat. He fingered the trigger and waited.

"Here, chicky-chicky," resumed the voice, now quivering with ill-disguised delight.

Instinctively, Esmond ducked, and the tongue of flame passed over his head. He fired without aiming. The bullet hit the wall and ricocheted. The dragon hiccuped, swallowing its flames. There was a commotion in the stairwell, the sound of someone falling down hard, and a loud curse.

"*Scheisse!*"

It was the same voice as before, now speaking its native language.

"*Ich komm' dich holen, mein Schatz...* I'm coming to get you, my treasure," cooed the voice. As Esmond beat a retreat, the inferno came to life again, igniting the staircase steps and scorching the walls.

Taking just enough time to signal the girl to stay hidden, Esmond raced up the last flight of stairs two at a time. The flame-thrower was now roaring continuously. Esmond braced himself against the last steps in the hope of repeating his earlier exploit, but the heat forced him to jump back and take cover in a hollow in the wall. Sweat was running down his forehead. He wiped it off with the back of his hand, not realizing that he was also ripping out a hank of hair and strips of dead skin. He looked at the sky for the last time, and saw that the sun had finally started to shine through the clouds. Far in the distance, he heard the sounds of fighting redouble in intensity. Then flames obliterated the sky, reaching the peak of the tower and casting a reddish glow on the bronze bell. Esmond spun round and rushed toward the top of the stairwell. Through the choking waves of heat, he now glimpsed his adversary's square face, the black beret with the death's head, the fierce, staring eyes. The jet of flames passed a few inches from his hip. With the advantage of surprise, Esmond grabbed the flame-thrower's metal nozzle and shoved it upwards. A lacerating pain flooded him as the red-hot metal scorched his palm. He screamed, and his scream joined that of the man in black, who was now a human torch tumbling backwards down the stairs. Esmond fell to the ground with his burned hand dangling uselessly at the end of his arm.

He must have passed out, because when he came to, armed men were kneeling around him, bandaging his hand. He glimpsed the little girl's face as she leaned over him, and he opened his mouth to speak. One of the men signaled him to rest.

"You're in good hands. The Fascists fell back."

"My friends…?" breathed Esmond.

The man hesitated, then, lowering his eyes, shook his head.

Eric's right hand, clutching the mouse, was sore. He rubbed it, not yet quite aware of where he was. Charles was pounding his shoulder and pointing to the screen, where a series of numbers and percentages were displayed. Eric closed his eyes, remaining for a few moments longer Esmond Romilly, age nineteen, sole survivor of the second company of the 12th Thaelmann International Brigade battalion.

"You won!" Charles was saying, incredulous. "You won! You eliminated Andreas!"

"I know," said Eric.

He opened his eyes, now shining with tears, and tore himself away from the life that had been his, a life he knew would end in a Canadian Air Force plane over the Atlantic in 1942. He swore he would live a better life, in memory of Esmond Romilly, Tich Adderley, and all the others.

When his unit's insignia appeared onscreen, Eric switched off the computer.

"What time is it?" he asked.

"Nine thirty," said Charles.

"Call Andreas, find out how he's doing."

They tried, but nobody answered.

26

He would show them.

Some day, he would show them all what he could do.

With just one gesture, he would wipe away their stupid smiles, their giggling, even the memory of his defeat.

It had taken Andreas weeks to recover from the last session, to repress the memory of those seconds of horror when the flames engulfed him, burning his lips and eyelids and flowing down into his lungs. He had finally died, crumpled at the foot of the ruined church stairs, and had awakened lying on the floor of his bedroom, soaked with tears and urine. Onscreen, the condor image had just finished burning up.

Eric had tried several times to talk to him over the following days, but Andreas cut off any attempt at conversation. He didn't want to give Eric the chance to crow over his victory. Eric had humiliated him, destroyed him, and enjoyed doing it. One day Andreas would take revenge. In the meantime, he feigned indifference and detachment. But he followed Eric and his friends from a distance, spying on them, without their ever noticing him.

Eric and Charles were always hanging out together now. He saw them sometimes swapping game diskettes in class, but he also caught them more than once having long conversations over a book at the library. On the weekends, they would occasionally go out with Elena and Gilles. Andreas trailed them from afar, enjoying the fact that they weren't aware of him. Gilles walked without looking where he was going; he had eyes only for the Bosanski princess. They were made for each other, those two; it made you want to puke. And Eric didn't seem to resent this budding romance. No surprise there; he never did have what it took to hang onto a girl, and certainly not enough balls to punch out his brother...

Murderous fantasies preyed on Andreas. He imagined running all four of them down with a racing car, or else killing them one by one, so as to fully enjoy the agony of the survivors. Who would he start with? Charles, of course... or maybe the Bosanski princess.

He hated them, and everything he saw or heard on television or the radio fed that hatred. Here, a politician railing against foreigners, blaming them for France's economic failures and unemployment. There, a once-famous actress who had taken up the cause of animal rights was condemning Muslims as fanatical invaders and sheep slaughterers... The tracts and magazines his father brought home spoke endlessly of the cleansing violence to come, of the supremacy of the white race, of the revenge to be taken by a beleaguered nation. Feeding on that hate, Andreas gradually became convinced that it was justified by a series of race-related news events. Immigrant hostels firebombed in Germany, speeded-up deportations from France... He took all those events to be the forerunners of some great, future Armageddon, in which he fervently hoped to take part.

Overcoming his dislike of books, Andreas had found in his father's bookcase a number of leather-bound volumes decorated with military coats of arms in gilt. They transported him into a mythic universe inhabited by blond warriors, men in uniform marching in serried ranks, their flags snapping in the winds of history. The very titles of the books made him shiver, titles like *The Waffen S.S.*, *Hitler Youth*, *A Life of Service to the Führer*, *The Russian Front*, *Stalingrad*. There were other books, too, with less showy covers and briefer text, if any. In page after page, photo after photo, you could see what Nazi Germany's great design had been: the creation of a master race free of refuse and detritus.

Andreas enjoyed leafing through the collections of posters from those days, where you could see reproductions of large drawings of the different races that inhabited the Earth: cowardly, apathetic blacks; greedy, hunchbacked Jews, huddled over their money and hiding their grossly caricatured features — hooked nose, bulging eyes, greasy hair — under ridiculous guises; and tall, blond Aryans, with short hair, blue eyes, and a commanding gaze. He would glance up from the pages of these books to look at himself in the mirror, unconsciously straightening up, puffing out his chest, and clench-ing his jaw, finding in his reflection the proof that he, too, was one of the elect, an *Ubermensch*.

In class, while Maffioli, Levine (that was a Jew-ish name, wasn't it?), and the other fools droned on with their lectures, Andreas enjoyed examining his classmates' faces in turn, to identify their racial type. How many of them could boast of belonging to the Aryan race, like him? A thin smile slowly spread across his face as he sat in the back of the class near the radiator, his eyes slitted, imagining what their fate would be when the long-awaited Armageddon finally arrived.

Other images occurred to him, images that had taken root in his mind and inflamed his imagination ever since he discovered them in his father's books. Images of raids; of Jewish children, their eyes full of fright, shoved into freight trains by powerful, proud soldiers; of ragged resisters propped against a wall and machine-gunned by a victorious German army; of haggard skeletons in striped uniforms dragging themselves through the mud of concentration camps. Andreas had learned the camps' names by heart, and recited them to himself in a kind of litany: Auschwitz-Birkenau, Bergen-Belsen, Chelmno, Treblinka. Closing his eyes, he could see his enemies in the middle of that crowd of the living dead: Gilles, Eric, Charles, and the Bosanski bitch. He imagined himself as a uniformed soldier whipping one across the face or playing Russian roulette against another's temple. Only his teachers' frequent rebukes could snap Andreas out of his daydreams. At times, he had even been sent to the principal's office to sit through some pointless lecture.

To calm his nerves, Andreas spent long hours roaming the corridors of *Doom* and *Rise of the Triad*, spattering the screen with blood and guts. But that soon became meaningless. Andreas the Fragmeister had tasted the ultimate experience, the game of war, and those poor imitations paled by comparison. More than anything else, he hated Eric for having permanently cut him off from that fascinating world, of which, for a short time, he had been the unchallenged master.

Finally, the day came when, unable to stand it anymore, Andreas started building his bomb.

He methodically assembled the components, taking care not to leave any clues in the various stores where he bought what he needed, household products that aroused no suspicion.

He first experimented with weak charges, then stronger ones. For a while, he was satisfied to fool around with jerry-built devices out in the woods. But now the stakes were higher, now it was a matter of an act that would make the front pages of the newspapers and magazines. With a firecracker, a sugar cube, and a cigarette, he had managed to paralyze the school for half a day. Nobody could imagine the impact this master stroke would have.

One evening when he was in his bedroom, putting the final touches on his trigger mechanism, a violent thunderstorm blacked out the entire neighborhood. Andreas was careful not to strike a match, since his room now reeked of gasoline and chemicals, a smell that didn't seem to overly concern his father. He groped his way to the door and went down to the ground floor to reset the circuit breakers. On his second try, the lights went on. He went back upstairs and shut himself in his room. The computer, which he had been using to jot down his thoughts over the last weeks, was running.

Andreas stared at the screen, on which flames were now flickering. A powerful, familiar voice rang in his ears: "Choose your game mode."

Astonished, Andreas sat down at his desk, swept his supplies aside, and seized the mouse. He had already tried more than once to run *The Ultimate Experience*, even going as far as reinstalling the game from the original diskette. Nothing had worked. He could never access the game's startup screens. And now suddenly what he had hoped for most was happening. Andreas didn't bother to ask why. He wasn't even surprised to hear his speakers working, though they had given up the ghost one evening two months before, when he had cranked to the max a pirate recording of a Dutch Nazi rock group.

Andreas clicked on the screen and immediately chose "Ultimate" mode. A menu of choices appeared. He clicked on "Twentieth Century," then on "1936–1939."

"Access denied," said the voice.

Worried — and furious at being reminded of his earlier failure — Andreas chose "1939–1945." To his great relief a new menu appeared, listing place names, battles, and wartime events. He grunted, deeply satisfied. Pearl Harbor, Stalingrad, Warsaw, Dachau... As the list scrolled by, Andreas fairly twitched with impatience. He clicked feverishly at a

173

screen that listed the dozens of units he could choose from: S. A., S. S., Wehrmacht, Condor Legion, Gestapo…

He made his selection, the CPU whirred, and the image appeared of a Paris street early in the morning. In the distance crowd noises, police whistles, and a bus honking its horn could be heard. Andreas crossed the street to look at his reflection in a clothing store window. He was tall, with short hair, wearing a black trench coat and boots. Intensely pleased, he started walking toward the town square, pausing only to glance at the date on the newspapers at a kiosk: July 16, 1942…

When he reached the square, which was cordoned off by police, Andreas could hardly contain his joy. City buses crammed with men, women, and children were parked along the sidewalk. Damp fingers had left their mark on the steamed-up windows. The police were checking the papers of everyone caught in their net, silently and conscientiously separating the crowd into two groups. Most of those who escaped the roundup hurried home, their eyes downcast, to vanish into their doorways. Only a few passers-by stopped and stared intently at the scene, as if to brand it on their memories.

Among the latter, Andreas noticed a young man of about fifteen wearing a windbreaker, who was feverishly examining the faces crowded behind the bus windows. Andreas slipped along the wall, slowly approaching him. The boy must have felt he was being watched, because he turned and looked at Andreas, who glanced down for a moment, pretending to be interested in a store window. When he looked up again, his prey was far away. Retreating from the crowd of policemen, the boy rushed down a side street. Andreas started to run and saw him enter a broken-down building. He followed him into the building and raced up the stairs in the darkness. They reached the top floor together. The grimy panes in the casement windows didn't let in much light, but it was enough for Andreas to see the fear in his victim's eyes. I love this game! he thought.

"*Ausweis, bitte…*" he said, savoring each word.

The boy pulled his identity papers from his windbreaker and held them out to Andreas, who smiled when he saw the word "Jew" on the document.

"*Warum tragen Sie nicht Ihren Stern?*" he demanded in a tone that couldn't hide his feeling of triumph.

The boy didn't answer. He remained motionless, trembling, looking at the floor. For an instant, Andreas had the feeling he had seen him before, but where? It wasn't Charles, or Eric, or Gilles. And yet he was sure of it…

"Why aren't you wearing your star?" he repeated.

When the boy didn't reply, Andreas grabbed him by the arm and pushed him toward the stairs, muttering:

"Verdammter Jude."

He escorted his captive to the main square, glowering at the few witnesses who seemed to show any disapproval, and walked up to a police official.

"Officer, this one was trying to escape…"

He held out the boy's papers, and waited while the policeman read them.

"But he's barely fifteen years old."

"You aren't aware of the orders?" Andreas barked. "We're rounding everybody up, even the children."

He laughed, at which the policeman backed away. Andreas brushed by him, still dragging the boy by the sleeve. He walked to the door of an already crowded bus and shoved the boy in.

"Bon voyage!" he shouted, loudly enough to be heard over the noise of the crowd.

"It will never end," the boy murmured to him in a kind of farewell. The bus started and pulled away, leaving Andreas standing stock-still on the sidewalk.

It was the old man, he realized; the old man from the shop… Andreas was still trying to figure out what this meant when a hand tapped him on the shoulder. He turned to hear, "Your papers sir, please."

Andreas hesitated, mystified by the mistake, then chose to smile. He straightened and took his official papers from his pocket, anticipating the look that would appear on the cop's face when he realized his error. He held his papers out politely, almost obsequiously.

"Why aren't you wearing your star?" the officer asked.

Andreas opened his mouth to speak, but only a strangled hiccup came out. His face flushed.

"You must be out of your mind! You think I'm Jewish, is that it? I belong to the S.S.! I'm here to supervise…"

"Cut the jokes, Mr. Salaun," the policeman said. "Please come with me."

"But I'm a member of the S.S., I tell you!"

"Nice try," answered the officer, who was now surrounded by three other policemen. "But this is strictly a French police operation, and these papers are obvious forgeries. Get in and don't make any trouble."

"But I'm not *Jewish*!" Andreas screamed as they seized him and pushed him aboard, shoving him into the sea of shattered humanity.

He was seething with rage and shame at the idea of being mistaken for a Jew by those idiots. Then the bus started, and Andreas began the first stage of his long journey into darkness. Terror overwhelmed him. The terror soon erased the shame, which itself became only a memory, and the least of his worries.

— THE END —

About the Author

CHRISTIAN LEHMANN was born in Paris in 1958, and now works as a practicing physician, in addition to writing for the press, the movies, and television. The author of four adult novels and seven children's books, Christian Lehmann lives near Paris. *Ultimate Game,* his first novel to be translated into English, won three literary prizes, including the Prix Lecture Jeunesse.

About the Translator

WILLIAM RODARMOR has translated nine other French books, including three for David Godine. His translation of *Tamata and the Alliance* by Bernard Moitessier won the 1996 Lewis Galantière Award from the American Translators Association.

Ultimate Game

was set in a digital version of Electra, a type originally designed by William Addison Dwiggins for the Mergenthaler Linotype Company and first made available in 1935. Electra is impossible to classify as either "modern" or "old-style." Not based on any historical model or reflecting any particular period or style, it is notable for its clean and elegant lines, its lack of contrast between thick and thin elements that characterizes most modern faces, and its freedom from all idiosyncrasies that distract the eye from reading.

The book was designed by Mark Polizzotti.